WHEN
WE WERE
BIRDS

stories

MARIA MUTCH

Published by Simon & Schuster
New York   London   Toronto   Sydney   New Delhi

SIMON &
SCHUSTER
CANADA

Simon & Schuster Canada
A Division of Simon & Schuster, Inc.
166 King Street East, Suite 300
Toronto, Ontario, M5A 1J3

Acknowledgment is made to Jonathan Cott for permission to reprint excerpts from his book *Conversations with Glenn Gould* © Jonathan Cott.

Ovid quotes (pages vii and 33), *The Metamorphoses of Ovid,* trans. Mary M. Innes (Penguin Classics, 1955); copyright © Mary M. Innes, 1955. Reproduced by permission of Penguin Books, Ltd.

Permissions are listed on page 233, which is considered a continuation of the copyright page.

This Simon & Schuster Canada edition April 2018

SIMON & SCHUSTER CANADA and colophon are trademarks of Simon & Schuster, Inc.

For information about special discounts for bulk purchases, please contact Simon & Schuster Special Sales at 1-800-268-3216 or CustomerService@simonandschuster.ca.

Interior design by Carly Loman

Manufactured in the United States of America

10   9   8   7   6   5   4   3   2   1

Library and Archives Canada Cataloguing in Publication

Mutch, Maria
[Short stories. Selections]
When we were birds : stories / by Maria Mutch.
Issued in print and electronic formats.
ISBN 978-1-5011-8279-2 (hardcover).—ISBN 978-1-5011-8280-8 (ebook)
I. Title.
PS8626.U885A6 2018   C813'.6   C2017-904197-5
                                          C2017-904198-3

ISBN 978-1-5011-8279-2
ISBN 978-1-5011-8280-8 (ebook)

"You will be sorry you did not give me it!" he cried, and flung himself over a high cliff. Everyone thought that he had fallen, but he was changed into a swan, and hovered in the air on snowy wings.

—OVID, *METAMORPHOSES*

WHEN
WE WERE
BIRDS

CONTENTS

two stories about **glenn gould**

part I

Plate II.

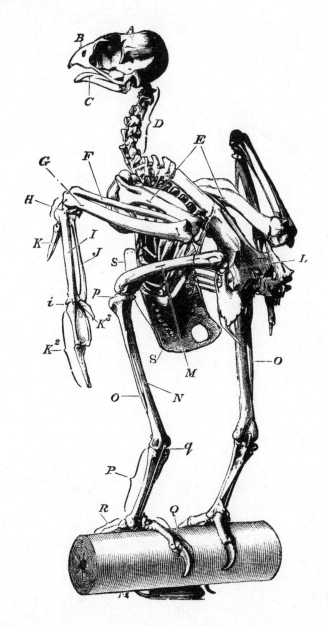

THE PEREGRINE

AT THE END OF THE WORLD

Love here requires the savage offering, something wrecked by talons and a beak, it requires staking out a claim forty stories up. He brings his mate pigeons he has plucked clean, mourning doves, a duck. (They copulated, balanced on the edge of the building, even after the eggs were laid, just because.)

His fledglings were born during a stormy April and now, at the top of the city, the peregrine must teach them the hunt. His daughter paces the edge of the rooftop, furious with hunger. He baits her with a half-dead pigeon, dropping it in the chasm between the mirrored bank towers and office buildings in which they sometimes mistake themselves for enemies. On the street below: the rushing suits, some baby strollers, a tourist ruining the picture.

The daughter plunges, hitting the pigeon, then circles up and back for another strike, and once more with a taloned clutch.

Her prize is limp in her grasp when she lands on a corner ledge of the Stedman building, not far from the fortieth floor where two window cleaners are dangling. The men work several feet apart, without a platform, using harnesses and ropes, their buckets secured to the right of their bosun's chairs. She doesn't mind their presence as she is more concerned with her hectoring siblings; she fixes the pigeon under her claw and scans to see where they are.

Thom sweeps his scrubber across the glass and returns it to his bucket to grab his squeegee in a gesture that finds him in his sleep; sometimes he dreams that his squeegee slips from his fingers and he watches as it hurtles murderously to the sidewalk. Even with the anxiety, he likes his job—the weird freedom of suspension high up, the trance-inducing art of cleaning the glass so that it bears the least trace of his sweep—even if the hazards, which at the moment include procreating falcons, are various. The window cleaners and the peregrines have hashed out a tacit understanding regarding their comings and goings, and as long as the cleaners obey the rules and allow the windows around the nest to remain grimy, everything goes smoothly.

Each winter the same two peregrines return to inspect the pea-gravel-filled nesting box, which sits in one of the Stedman's deep window wells and is overseen by the conservation society, and hash out their plans for spring delivery. Thom has watched three seasons so far of the Apollo and Daphne story, aided by the live-streamed video of the box and an online debate about whether or not the pair would return to the same spot this year. Season one Apollo and Daphne had two chicks, who grew up and moved to the next borough, season two they had three chicks, one of which died when it fell into a space around the nesting box—after which the box was remade to prevent another occurrence—and season three is the current one, with another three offspring, named Clyde, Mercy, and Persephone (he hasn't been able to figure out the naming strategy; two of last year's chicks were Nik and Pik). He believes that he can tell Persephone from her siblings, being convinced that she is slightly larger than the other two and sporting an unusual light-colored patch on her mantle, but the other cleaners tell him he's dreaming. Chuck, the oldest and stoutest of the cleaners, snorted out his coffee and said, "Christ, Thom. They just some fowl. Probably not delicious neither."

Thom sweeps the glass, then adjusts his ropes to descend another few feet so that he is almost level with Danny, two windows over. They can see into one of the offices and two of the people get up from their desks and leave, possibly because the dangling men make them nervous. Sometimes people do that or sometimes they like to watch and will even wave, and one woman on the twentieth floor has been known to hold up short messages: *hey handsome* or *you missed a spot*. One day last year a zaftig woman in one of the law offices flashed her breasts at them, which prompted Danny to say, "You know, I appreciate that." He gave her a thumbs-up.

The wind is stronger today than the cleaners anticipated, which sends streaks of water across some of the windows they've already done. Thom can see one of the adult peregrines riding the thermals, effortless, searching for prey, and Persephone, who has her captive tight in her grasp as she works at it. The pigeon has a dull look, as if a shade has been drawn across its eye, though it appears cognizant somehow that its torso is being shredded. It seems to be breathing as Persephone's beak wrecks at the feathers, pulling up sinews and bits that snap away like elastics.

He wishes Danny would say something. His partner likes to talk about his girlfriend most of all, followed by soccer, followed by some of the things they see. He keeps an unwritten list of the wonders: office shenanigans, sudden weather, even the light on the buildings in late afternoon and the strange perspective of being so high up, which neither of them ever really gets used to. He likes to bring up *that guy*. "You remember that guy," he'll say. Thom hates talking about it at the same time that he is relieved that one other person in his life knows about *that guy*.

Thom had been at the job for only three months when he and Danny were cleaning the fifty-fourth floor of one of the neighboring buildings, one entirely in glass and steel, ninety stories, a glimmery, slippery megalith that looks almost liquid when the cleaning is fresh and the work has been windless. There was the man on the fifty-seventh floor, just an office worker at an office party. Demonstrating, the news sites later said, the effectiveness of the windows' strength, their impenetrability, by throwing his body against the glass. Once, and then again, bam. Laughing maybe. *See that? Nobody gets out through the windows, that's for sure!* None of which Thom or Danny could have been aware of. Then one more slam and what they saw above them and to the side was the impossible, the silent opening of a five-by-ten-foot plate of glass as it came away from its seal, the slow eeriness as it sailed out, and the man with it, into the cold, shadowy space between the buildings. The man and the glass fell as though floating, not unlike the peregrines riding the currents, as if not entirely affected by gravitational forces. The man fell, Danny would later say, as if it was okay with him—he didn't even scream. But they both understand that the way they saw the man fall and the way the man actually fell were two different things, that what they saw was really a trick of the mind, of the hearing, the only thing they could possibly walk away with.

Thom and Danny's boss made them take a few days off, and for a while after they got back to work nobody mentioned the man, until one day Danny made him into shorthand for the hapless. "She walked out, Thomas. I open the door and whammo! She's gone, her shit's gone. She even took the fridge magnets. The magnets! That's what a cold bitch she is. Literally, I did not see that shit coming. You know?—like *that guy*." He made a gesture with his hand, drawing an arc in the air. "Whammo."

So the birds. The magnificent peregrines. Thom is grateful when the birds are around the nest, living their lives up where the men are working. Their grace reminds him to be careful of his lines and equipment, to take nothing for granted; their savagery reminds him to toughen up.

He found out that peregrine chicks are called eyasses, and when they hatched, he was upset, despite having seen this two times before, that members of the society, in partnership with Crystal Clean Inc. so they could use some of the cleaners' equipment to reach the box, came to band the shaggy youngsters. Apollo and Daphne, sporting their own leg bands, made wild, furious swoops, even knocking the hard hat off one of the conservationists. But after that excitement, after the eyasses got their bands and were safely back where they belonged, the scrape was calm again. Eventually the siblings lost their shagginess and began to look more like their parents. They started making short flights, Clyde and Mercy first, watched stonily by Persephone, who followed several days later.

The peregrines are wanderers, with vast ranges, but they seem to love the Stedman; there is also a church nearby with inviting ledges and carvings around the base of the steeple where they like to perch. He watches as Persephone, in a bid to avoid the encroaching flights of her siblings, brings her pigeon to sit on one of St. Ignatius's stone angels. She glowers out—almost, he thinks, right at him—two winged creatures atop another. From this angle the pigeon appears resigned, utterly subjugated to its own dismantling; even disconcertingly cooperative. When he finally glances away, the mechanical jabs of Persephone's beak are still in his mind.

In spite of the sometimes ferocious, sometimes quizzical arrangement of their faces and their status as fastest animal, the peregrines have a fragility that has on occasion rattled his sleep. He would never tell Danny or the others, but sometimes he sits in the fifth pew of St. Ignatius and makes his appeals for another good year for Apollo and Daphne, in the hopes that his prayers, his old-fashioned keening, are some kind of atonement for what happened decades earlier: the peregrines' endangerment by the DDT-induced thinness of their eggshells. Not that he is personally responsible, but he feels regret all the same. He looks again at Persephone, who seems interested in him as he dangles there. From her vantage, he appears to smooth away his image then make it reappear. The wind catches his seat and swings him out a little from the building, so he grabs his suction cups and anchors himself to the glass.

Hers is not the sort of face that would accept an apology, he thinks. His online group has reminded him numerous times when he's gotten fired up that the replenishment programs around the country have been a story of success, redemption even, and the peregrines have adapted, replacing their craggy cliffs with office buildings and a feed of urban pigeons, sparrows, flickers, and the occasional squirrel. But he doesn't share their optimism. The man falling out of the window and last year's chick falling into the space beside the nest are reminders to him of the possibilities, as if dangling into a void by ropes and pulleys is not already knowledge enough.

That very morning, his mother had texted him, yet again: **please quit** ☺, but he has no intention. Some of the guys on the team have been doing this twenty years. He has tried telling her about having a front-row seat to the peregrines, to the poor sods working in the offices. He's told her, "Ma, it's beautiful up there." He has tried to describe how, when he looks down, he sees tourist buses and eighteen-wheelers round corners with almost the same smooth movement as the peregrines when they ring up toward prey. He tried another tack: How many people, he asked her, get to rappel up and down the sides of buildings like comic book heroes? How many get to dangle far above people and their problems, or outside of them? Not many, he told her, not many.

Out of the corner of his eye, he catches movement and looks to see Persephone lift off from the stone angel. The pigeon—whatever was left of it—is gone, and then Persephone, too. It happens suddenly, the way she disappears. One moment she is there gliding through that openness, what he privately calls the blue space, and he is admiring her near-adult silhouette, the smoothly pointed wings, the way her talons are tucked away, and the next moment she curves by an office tower farther down the block and disappears. Just like that, she is gone.

odysseys

The man tells the clerk at the bank that he's looking for his wife, that he's been looking for a long time. Paul, the clerk, eyes him over the counter, notes the disheveled canvas coat—expensive and inappropriate for the current weather, with a striped shirt underneath. The man fiddles with the chain on the ballpoint pen while he speaks, filling the marble canyon of the old bank with his consternations, how he has been spending his days looking in cafés and shops and banks, even under the smelly slopes of bridges, feeling the cold mud in his Gucci shoes and the drooping gaze of the drug addicts as he shows them her photograph. He even warmed his hands by the lit barrel, before tossing bills to the men with plastic bags emerging from their shoes, and climbing back up the knoll to the car waiting for him. He has repeated this pattern, he tells Paul, for more days than he can count, and someone told him that perhaps she is working here, perhaps Paul knows something and can tell him where he might find her, Eugenia, his wife. He says that his name is Stedman. Garth T. Stedman.

Paul screws his lips to one side while he thinks and watches the man, and Syed has finished with his customer and is leaning in slightly to hear better. Snow melts on the man's shoulders, staining him, and his hair is a stiff, windblown tuft that only someone crazy or genius can pull off, his signet ring snags the light pouring down from the vaulted ceiling's iron chandeliers. Whether he is really her husband or not—and she never mentioned a partner—Paul cannot assess, but it makes no difference.

"Except that I don't know where she is," he says. "She worked here, then she quit, weeks ago." It occurs to him to mention the pigeon incident, but he decides to hold that spectacle inside himself—how marvelous to witness a savage like that, as if prehistory had suddenly sprung up right there in front of him—not something you see everyday, and possibly not something to tell this man, who looks as though he wouldn't understand. "I would love to help you," says Paul, "but I haven't heard from her. Her number doesn't work, and she seems to have moved. Nobody knows where she is or where to send her last paycheck . . . And, by the way, she prefers Percy." He winces a little seeing the look on the man's face, the pouched eyes, the hollowed cheeks. But her absence is the truth—he hasn't heard from her; of all the people he knows, she is probably the one most capable of wholly vanishing and never turning up again.

The man is not used to the negations of a bank clerk, but searching has made him tired and permanently creased, so much so that he is numb to the realization that he has found, if not his wife or the sense of her presence, then a place where someone at least knew her. He should have been ecstatic. The police have been useless, as have the investigators he has hired, and so here he is, fulfilling the adage about doing something yourself if you want it done right. Only now, the grey of a dead end. Perhaps, in some small way, he is afraid to find her, though this thought is contradicted by his efforts. He hasn't changed his clothes in days, gone to the office, or the club. The backseat of his car is obscured by food wrappers, bottled water, and a stack of clean clothes he has yet to change into. "Well, you tell her if you see her," he says, "you tell her I came in."

"Righto," says Paul, and he watches as the man turns on his expensive heel, forcing up the rumply edges of his coat, and heads for the door.

crumbs

He has been searching since June. Each building he enters he thinks might have contained her or someone who knows her, and every street he walks down becomes a place that could be marked by unseen traces of her, footprints, some stray hairs, the crumbs of her favorite coffee cake. He assumes, because it is comforting to do so, that she hasn't left the island and he has spent countless hours in the museums, riding the trains, combing the parks, and the public library, too, walking the stacks or even resting in the protective shadow of the lions. A hundred times he has thought that she is up ahead, turning to cross near Penn or hail a cab or enter a shop, but these pieces of her—the hair, the nose, the way of walking—never become the whole. He lacks the power to make the pieces coalesce into the real thing. He has even screamed her name—because that is an alchemy that sometimes works, the bellowed summons—when he was drunk and about to pour himself over the edge of his sister's uptown balcony, but she didn't materialize. For a moment he thought that she was there in the doorway, wearing her bathrobe, coming toward him—yes, coming toward him!—when it was only his sister, and the unanswered summons floated out, growing delicate until finally dusting the steaming roofs and water tanks and antennae.

Searching has filled his pockets and briefcase with photocopies of her face, until he got the idea to have the image printed on cards, heavy stock with rounded corners, by the same company that makes his business cards and letterhead, so that he carries a deck and doles them out in a way that reminds him of trading hockey cards when he was a boy. *I'll give you Ken Dryden and Yvan Cournoyer for Guy Lafleur, I'll give you more money than you've ever dreamed of if you tell me where she is.* Just like the films he watched when he had time for films. Close-up of unknown sweating face, fingers bunching up their lapels, *You tell me where she is!*

All he has is a note saying:

> *so beautiful and vicious, in a way, you know, though it is all*
>   *instinct*
> *and no other way to live but by the stoop and slam of bodies*
>   *into a meal, this is*
> *not the way to be anymore, at the top of the world, darling,*
> *don't you see, the end is coming as it must to save the world*
> *but not the one you think I am I am I am,*

and the paper, crisp as the day she wrote on it, which he has kept hidden from the investigators because they will think she's insane or gone of her own volition, is folded into hard quarters and kept in his safe.

Searching has even changed the shape of his body in these

last few weeks, as he has never walked so much in his life. Perhaps he has lost, along with her—the weight and the presence of her—another fifteen pounds, so that his clothes, even the Thomas Pink shirts and Desmond Merrion suits, make him look smelly and adrift. She would have been delighted to see him slender, as she was always feeding him kale and Brussels sprouts and a green drink redolent of sour ponds. In those last days, she had said that she could hear the elevator, the private one that turned up in their penthouse foyer, and that it had started to sound like bowing, like a cello, and sometimes like a shrieking bird. It meant absolutely nothing to him and in the morning her side of the bed was cool and the absence already pleating there told him things were going to be different.

He resolves to keep looking, of course. It feels like a new profession. He could do it forever, perhaps, pad along the streets at all hours, crunching the winter salt under his shoes or avoiding the urine puddles in spring. He will return to the bank, again and again, until Paul becomes weary or can be bought. He will carry one of her sweaters with him, an alpaca cardigan gone pilly from his snuffles and gropings into the grey weave. He will inhale the particles of her that swim in the net of it, as if she has been caught and held: as if.

persephone

When it happened it was early summer and the sidewalks held the day's heat. She felt the concrete with her hands for the first time. Transformation being a prickly subject for most, it isn't something

she is likely to mention. Her identification says Eugenia Elisabeth Stedman, but since when does one's identification speak the truth of it? She asks to be called Persephone, or, since that has a certain unwieldiness, Percy (and truth be told she has no real affinity for Persephone, only that it does seem to speak to the vertical shift in her circumstances).

She unfolded her limbs on a quiet street not far from the Stedman and Washington Square, and found that in the first few movements she was not strong on her feet. Like a doe, she wobbled. There weren't many people around at that hour and the ones that were ignored her. She was only a well-dressed drunk, and there were always plenty of those. When she was ready, when the amoebic slipperiness of being born or waking fell away, she planted one leather-clad foot, then the other. She pulled her shoulder blades back, wingless. It took her some time to adjust her vision as, she quickly realized, she no longer had the advantage of three images. She could, however, read the print on the crushed beer can thirty feet away and smell the roasted quail that the French restaurant had served two days before.

That was in June, and now it is December. Snow falls on the shoulders of people passing, it lands on the pavement and vanishes, more lands and sticks. She watches the crystals clump, tumble, and it is twilight and the lights of the restaurants and shops turn amber. She feels a snowflake land in her eye, no nictating membrane to sweep the cornea. The insides of buildings still fascinate her. As a peregrine, she had watched the glass towers as night was coming; the interiors and the people living within them were merely facets of the glass, particles that caused shimmerings and refractions that had to be ignored in favor of zeroing in on prey.

She has adapted well, she thinks, considering. She stocks her refrigerator with various undressed chickens, pigeons, and French hens, and she has moved on to rabbits, sometimes squirrels, and little else. She invited the man she was seeing to stay for two weeks solid—only an experiment—and he observed to his mother, "It's like living with a coyote." She prefers her lovers to be small in stature, and quick; also, disinclined to comment. Also, not actually residing in her apartment, which she has obtained with a false name and Eugenia's cash.

She is still unused to her body, though it has its perks. One minute she delights in it, and the next she mourns her bird form. The force that placed her on the sidewalk seems not to work in reverse. She can mutter her prayers to whatever mechanism converted her, but she remains decidedly human. She feels this most in her chest—she misses the comparative grandeur of her sternum, for instance, which previously held the muscular base for her wings—and her bones, which no longer hold small pockets of air. But what she misses most, of course, are the wings themselves, what she sees now is their wild sprawl, and the ability to compress herself into a tight, hurtling arrow, to slice the spaces where a pigeon dodders along, oblivious.

Nevertheless, the pleasures of fingers and feet and skin, scaleless legs, a soft mouth and clattery teeth, not to mention different sex organs, and breasts and everything forthwith, are considerable compensations at times.

Neither is it lost on her the ability to speak; when she lies in bed at night, she plays with pitch, alternating some of her favorite words with peregrine sounds. *Splendid* ih-ih-ih-ih *rancor* ih-ih-ih-ih-ih *vegetal* ihihihihi *fecund*. Until someone whacks an adjoining wall or bangs a broom handle on their ceiling.

Much of her prowess has come about because of her job at the bank, where she soaks up as many habits as possible, and blends in, she feels, almost seamlessly, with the exception of the fierce brow that her coworker Jen has suggested she Botox the hell out of. She has learned to ride the train beneath downtown's vespiary, and to take her clothing to a dry cleaner near her apartment (the man behind the counter always notes the rips and tears, the unraveling skirt hems, the blood-speckled plackets). She has learned to make lentil soup, to pick up lotto tickets, to tip the cab driver.

a meal

They invite her to a dinner party in their Chelsea apartment, the two coworkers who live together, Paul and Evan, and Sarah has insisted she come because she wants to figure her out, Syed has been wanting to ask her out, and Ming wants to know if she is stealing from the bank—not because this would be offensive, but because the information seems a powerful thing to have.

When Paul and Evan introduce their Shih Tzu, Mischa, to her, the little dog freezes, then trembles, dribbles a shiny urine coin on the sofa cushion before finally growling into the fun-fur guts of its pink teddy.

"Well, now," says Paul.

"She does that to everyone," says Evan. The Persian, Mui Mui, furiously mashes the carpet with its front paws before hissing and taking off for the bedroom.

She is delighted to be making some friends and revels in the habits of belonging to which she is becoming accustomed, the handshakes and clinking of glasses and kisses in the air. She adores this last one and thinks what a peculiar thing it is. Her coworkers' faces are so wonderfully lit by the numerous candles as they hold their wineglasses and cackle about the bank's CEO and his mistress habit. They toast her, and Syed says, "To our newest friend," which makes her smile. Paul is already pouring more wine for her, splashing some on the carpet when his mild cerebral palsy causes his hand to spasm, and Evan places the tray of canapés under her nose again, imploring her to take more, which she does only so that he will move along, solicit Amber and Joelle.

She marks the passing of time by the amount of wine being poured and the games they begin to play, ones involving cards or dice and lots of shrieking (it is hardest for her to tamp down the peregrine in her when she hears sounds approaching that of her family). She considers that, in spite of all the things she has learned to do, how far she has advanced in the last couple of months, she has been unable to curb the pigeon desire that boils up and now causes her to shift on the sofa where she has a plate of pasta balanced on her knee. She is sitting close to the kitchen where an open window is bringing in the winter air and on it the gamey, mossy smell of the pigeon that sits on the edge of the fire escape.

When the shrieking hits a high point and the plates have been scraped down, she edges closer to the kitchen, feigning a desire, perhaps, to fill her empty water glass. Night and the pigeon sit just beyond the window. A piece of the white curtain gets sucked under the sash and then released over and over. Snow blows in, glints on the sill. She watches the pigeon ruffling its feathers and shining in a way the others would not detect. She can feel the vibrations of the jittering heart, the stone grit mashing corn kernels and a bit of plastic in the gizzard, the mites feasting on skin. The pigeon plumbs its neck feathers with a slightly fissured beak emanating a scabrous smell, a wound three weeks old and crackling with dried blood. She catches a dribble of saliva on her chin, coughs into a paper napkin. She runs her hands under the tap and considers backing quietly out of the kitchen, grabbing her coat and racing home, perhaps picking off a squab or two in the park along the way. But their hearts are already locked together, their synaptic overlords already in talks to navigate how the stalking will play out, the pitch of her movement through the open window, the speed with which the pigeon will be snatched and to what extent it will acquiesce. Because one thing about the pigeon is that, in spite of its preoccupation with raking its breast plumage, it knows exactly who she is and that it hasn't got a chance.

Paul, with Evan coming up behind him, and followed by Amber, Sarah, and Syed, enters the kitchen and says, "We were wondering if you wanted to play euchre," except that only the first few words come out because Percy turns toward them with a red mouth. She clutches the pigeon in one fist and strokes her wrist across her chin to catch the blood. Tiny feathers are still in the air, waiting to land. She eyes them apologetically. Syed places his hands on Amber's shoulders as if she's a shield and says, "Wow."

"Yeah, wow," says Paul. Evan starts to giggle, which seems to catch until they all start laughing, louder and louder, and then finally Paul claps and then they all do. Percy stands there holding the bloody pigeon bundle, feeling its final wriggle, and she gives a little bow.

ovid's doing

Of course, the point of all this is not simply to be human. Call her a goddess, a shape-shifter, a creature of metamorphosis. And then some. Say that desire caused an outrageous condition. She suspects that the transition from one form to another is instinctive, like the cicadas bursting up every seventeen years or the migration of monarchs, and that her purpose is likewise wired in.

People might assume that someone with her function would spring from a raven or a crow—as they are harbingers, symbols,

and black—or even an albatross. She doesn't know what to consider herself. Even if she cannot seem to communicate with whatever made her a human, she knows the ugliness of her task, which makes her feel both energized and morose. So morose that sometimes she rides the elevators of the biggest buildings and goes to stand on the terraces and rooftops where snow accumulates in some of the corners. Looking out to the packed grid of buildings and lights, she contemplates the nature of existence, which she understands is an entirely human thing to do. She imagines the

Wild, though it is long gone, swallowed and disgorged as a city, but the people in the buildings have tried; they have planted some of the rooftops with pines and cedars and Blue Star junipers. Yet there are no cathedral forests, no haunted bogs where everything dies with one limb in the air. Even Central Park, held in such reverence by the humans, is no replacement. She looks to the sky, to the highest ledges and cornices to find the shapes of her mother, father, and siblings. Even with the vastness of their range, she occasionally catches glimpses of them, sometimes around the familiar cliff of the Stedman or sometimes miles away in Harlem.

So her purpose is lethal—she decides, after some thought, to call herself an Agent—and she has it without them. It is not so terrible a job to have, she supposes. She is dimly aware of other Agents in her area, one who was once an abandoned pit bull and another who had been a bat that flew headlong into a hanging bug zapper and bounced off with a new designation and purpose, but she cannot say exactly how she knows this.

In fact, though she has been looking solidly since taking on her new form she hasn't come across a single other person like her. She knows, she feels it in her human bones, that the animals who have undergone a similar transformation are legion and spreading. She understands, too, the mechanics; it is all in the fingertips, which makes her life in the city and her job at the bank ideal. She merely has to touch someone in passing, clip a shoulder or an elbow on the street for the connection to be made. She usually goes unnoticed and her victim continues on, but only for a while. She knows that death will come: perhaps a faulty brake system, unchewed bit of bread, virulent fever, malfunctioning wood chipper, loaded gun. She is merely the enabler.

She only wishes she knew them, the others, could exchange information with them. Get some affirmation for the weightiness of the task. The problem, as ever, is love. Both for the people she meets and for the peregrines. She wants to go back. She cranes her head to see the circles of her family on the bending air currents; her cellular call to the end of the world, apparently, has preceded theirs. Her mother is easier to pick out with human eyes because she's bigger than her father. She sees, sometimes, her brother and sister, she sees the dives, the floating, the suspension as they ride wind fifty, seventy stories up. She wonders if they consider where she might have gone or if they simply think she has wandered, as they all do, if they train their spectacular vision on the slopes of buildings looking for her.

transmission

When she first understood her task, she zealously touched as many humans as she could. Her coworkers, of course, are well taken care of, and any customer to the bank who shakes her hand or grazes her fingers when she gives out currency. So far none of her coworkers has met their demise, but this is not unexpected. Humans are always going on about how in the history of time and the universe, their occupation is representationally only a blink, but she knows the truth, which is that human time is long; too long, and death comes at a stroll, even when it appears otherwise. She walks through the city streets on her lunch breaks, bumping into people, making sure her fingers make contact when a coffee cup or a cronut is given to her. She has even pretended to greet someone she thinks she knows. It appears to people that she is klutzy, overly affectionate, a close-talker. Crazy. Her expectation is that the ones about to die feel no suspicion that their death is part of something larger. This is best, as anything else would lead to panic, and possibly, even, fighting back. What chaos there would be then. Glorious, maybe, but unhelpful to the cause.

This is all thrilling, in the beginning, the energy of it, the gist of revenge, and most especially that hallmark of extroversion: the touching. The touching! Marvelous to palpate the varieties of skins and callouses and twitching muscles, denim or wool or silk. Peregrines are so starved for this kind of thing. She grazes men in bars—what a plethora of death that is—or the nurses on a smoke break outside the hospital, even small children, though with so many protective parents, these are the biggest challenge and since she finds it unpleasant she often leaves them for the other Agents.

the proclaimers

In January, she makes her resolutions like everyone else, except that she resolves to find some of the others. At the end of the world, where most people are going about their business, there is the occasional person with a sign proclaiming it. Or rather, up ahead on one of her search expeditions, there is a single person sitting on a piece of cardboard on the icy concrete beside a drugstore. She sees that a few feet away from him is a large plastic doll with nails in its head, naked except for a decoupage of bottle labels, holding a sign that says: *the end of the world*. Only that, in black ink. The man is turned slightly away from the doll as if he has nothing to do with it.

"Are you one of them?" she asks him. "Do you know who I am?" He digs at the crusts of salt and ice with his hands and doesn't look up. She can hear him humming. People bump into her arm as they rush past, but she neither notices nor relishes her kills. She stares hard at the man, at his nearly bare scalp. She has an urge to kiss his skull because it seems to her oddly beautiful, but she stops herself.

"I think that's one of the most bizarre things anyone has ever walked up and said to me," he says, still digging. His fingernails are bloodied. "And I've heard a lot of shit."

She shoves her hands into the pockets of her overcoat, the letdown washing over her. He looks up and says, "Do *you* know who you are?"

"I need to find the others. I thought maybe you were one. It's so lonely. Don't you think?"

"Lady, I'm not sure what you want." He wipes his hands on his pant legs and she sees that he has an expensive watch, that his nails, even if bloodied, have been manicured. "I'm a performance artist. This is my gig, right? Other than that," he says, "I know nothing."

contagion

In February it happens that her extroversion begins to wear thin, and guilt, black as a scab, begins to form. She frowns more, furrowing that unplucked, obtruding brow, falls silent. Takes the wide-open route across the park, the unpopulated side streets. Uses the self-checkout, the unmanned subway entrance, sits in the vacant train car. She tells people she has a cold, slides money and bank slips across the counter with the tip of a pen, and then she stops going to work at all.

In her apartment at night she watches the cable news networks, trolling for the local epidemics, shootings, and storm surges that might, in an extrapolated way, be her influence. Though it won't make any difference now, she tells her current lover via text, and with the wording she learned early on from Sarah and Joelle: **It really isn't you. It's all me. Thx for everything.** She begins to wear latex gloves every single day.

She assumes that if there are others, there must be meetings, secret ones, where they would drink rum and Cokes in paper cups, perhaps, while sitting on folding chairs, and listen to others wander in and announce at the front of the room, *My name is* _____ *and I am an Agent of Death*. People would clap softly, maybe, or just nod. Commiseration would purr through the room like an electrical current, and between the mouthfuls of dry bagels or saltines she would learn where the others live, how they cope, if any of them has been able to change back to the thing they used to be.

On another of her search outings, she finds herself standing in front of an Eighth Avenue walk-up that purports to deal in environmental cleanup, wondering if this is where the people like her would hold meetings. Who was their leader, for instance, because surely they had one. What was the timeline, how successful were they so far, when is the date of the end times? All of these sound to her like reasonable questions. And she has suggestions to offer—why not have a website, brochures, a central telephone number for new recruits and as a means for acquiring new members? Calling cards in an attractive case? An Agents of Death listing? Although, if the potential acolytes are animals, as she was, they likely would not be perusing websites and calling phone numbers . . . But perhaps others had made a transition to the human only to discover a lack of clarity with regard to what they were supposed to be doing once they had opposable thumbs and apartment keys. Perhaps there were numerous others like herself, and perhaps they were also longing for the old world, the old form, the always being in the present moment, the thinking with feathers and talons and whiskers and fur, the embroilment in the never-ending task of the hunt. It is, she knows, a whole other way of operating.

When she rattles at the doors of the business and finds them locked, she decides to keep moving, her human flesh being so much more susceptible to cold. It is coffee she wants, even though she hasn't quite developed a taste for it. It is all another experiment, and she regards the cafés themselves and the waiting in line as pleasures; she will sip at the first inch of coffee, once she has it, reluctant to leave the line and its occupants, the mulling of the pastries and impatient shuffling, the sound of the odd coin hitting the floor.

As she waits to place her order, there are two teenage girls in front of her wearing what appear to be pajama bottoms and boots, and a middle-aged woman behind them who is packed into her sweater set tight as a grape, her puffer coat over her arm on account of the hot flash that Percy can detect from several feet away.

Both girls have their phones out. One says to the other, "If a guy sent you a text that said, 'I need you now,' what would you say, do you think?"

The other girl doesn't look up from her phone. "That's it? He just says, 'I need you now'? Apropos of what?"

"Not apropos of anything. No context. Just: 'I need you now.' That's it."

"What kind of need? Like, sexual?"

"Not sexual. Emotional."

The girl looks up so her friend can see her rolling her eyes. "I'd say, 'Ok, bye.'"

Percy has been listening intently. Sweater set can't help herself and unleashes a guffaw loud enough that the girls turn and look at her.

"My god, I love your generation—your hearts are the size of peas!" she shrieks, laughing into her hand. "It's magnificent, really, how mean you all are."

The girls smirk a little at each other. They wait for her to say something else and the woman obliges. "Well, it's all to the good. Your generation—of which, by the way, you two are fine examples—your generation is going to be the catalyst for the biggest thing there is. The End."

The girls look blankly at her, but Percy bristles with these last two words. Her heart starts pounding. The woman beams delight into the girls' open stare. "You know, the apocalypse. I know they don't teach you little twerps cursive anymore, but you do know about the End Times, yes?" She gestures with her hands and makes a sound like an explosion, except not a very good one. "Locusts, disease, whatever. But then comes the good part: we'll get to go up to heaven with Jesus!"

The girls start choking and snickering. The woman adds, "Except for you and your kind, of course. You'll have to stay here and pick through the splinters. You're going to need better boots."

The barista hands the girls their cups, which they can barely hold onto they're laughing so hard. "Ok, well, have fun up there then," one of them says, wiggling her fingers, and they leave the shop, leaning into each other as they stumble out.

The woman watches them go with a tight smile. She gets her coffee and Percy follows her out to the street, trailing ten feet behind, then more to be safe. She has spent the last weeks being so careful to touch no one, and yet she is quite certain that what she is doing now is stalking prey. Two days earlier, she had listened to a recording of the philosopher Alan Watts on her headphones and he had said something extraordinary, "You never were born and you never will die." He himself was dead, and yet there he was, right in her ears.

Her desire to interact with this woman is nearly overwhelming, as if the woman is emitting the scent of a pigeon. She stops to put on her coat and Percy stops also, pretends to rifle the bookrack outside a second-hand store.

They are moving again along the snowy sidewalks, and Percy can feel the pulse of energy in her fingertips. She has wondered if death is not a description of a state or event, but a measurable thing, if it might appear wriggly and alive under a microscope. Perhaps death has hidden attributes, chemicals, operations of the subatomic that remain undiscovered; perhaps there is even a sound when her hands make contact with a victim that, like a dog whistle, is detected only by certain creatures. She cannot help, after all, that those killing particles live inside her. At any rate, perhaps the act of touching (what she calls designating) is really a version of tending, like deadheading flowers in a musty garden.

Sweater set has picked up speed and is now half a block up ahead. Death tingles in Percy's fingers, and she starts to pant with how badly she wants to touch. The woman stops at a chirping parked car, removes a paper from the wiper blades and rips it into pieces that she sprinkles on the meter. Percy has allowed too much space between them and can't close the gap fast enough. The woman is in her car and then trying to nose into traffic. There is a barrage of honking and a grey bowl of exhaust that rises and rises.

Percy takes off her gloves and stands there, looking up. She wants to see against the top floors of an inky glassed building the shape of a peregrine gliding. She is staring upward so intently and for so long that other people feel compelled to glance skyward also, though none of them stop. They hustle forward without noticing her touch. Her telltale posture with the neck craned back and the mouth agape in wonder is only the mark of an outsider, and she is just another tourist, amazed by the spectacle of looking up.

The first victims were the countless birds, still spellbound by the voice of the singer, the snakes and the throng of wild animals, the audience which had brought Orpheus such renown. The frenzied women began by seizing upon these; then, with bloodstained hands, they turned on Orpheus himself, flocking together just as birds do, if they see the bird of night abroad by day. It was like the scene in an amphitheatre when, for a morning's entertainment in the arena, a doomed stag is hunted down by dogs.

—OVID, *METAMORPHOSES*

THE LOGIC OF LOSS

On a day in April 1999, Nicholas saw the white birds circling the park-
ing lot, descending to an invisible drain. People filled their trunks
with boxes and bags, the roof racks, too, they left shopping carts
thirty feet from the corrals where they caught the wind, clanged.
Nothing is simple and nothing is complicated; this was the sentence in his mind, the one on repeat, a koan for stealing a baby.
Nothing is complicated. He expected this day, however, to be
charged with unexpected delays and witnesses and jangled nerves.
Birds choked back wads of yarn and paper that drifted on the pavement, and music blared from speakers high up, though he couldn't
have said what the music was. His wife, Audrey, clutched the baby
and jerked across the lot, terror and glee affecting her limbs. He

thought she looked ridiculous, yet nobody was noticing anything except their keys in the locks, their tortilla chips and bleach and rubber spatulas trundled like riches. Nothing was garbage yet. The world was new and the detergent bottles hadn't yet been opened and the plastic beads were still unworn.

Nicholas put his hand on Audrey's back. The baby turned her head like an owl's, taking everything in as Audrey jiggled her toward the car. Babies, he knew, see who you are, but even though she looked straight at him with an expression that said she had him all figured out, she didn't make a fuss. She went along with the charade that they were a family like any other, that this was normal and fine and so was the car and the hazy light and the white birds. Where their friend Margaux was he didn't know, but he pictured her shimmying out of clothes, he pictured her running and tossing her glasses, he pictured her.

Everything was fine, except the baby had a lump on her neck and he thought he had noticed it in the store, but now that they were out in daylight, he was certain it was there, a small egg shape tight under the skin. Right below it, a tiny collar in white with pink rickrack, a pearl button. When she had been sitting in her mother's shopping cart near the tower of paper towels, she had swiped at her neck, then watched her own hands. Nicholas and Audrey had watched the baby from twenty feet away, pretended to discuss the sunscreen and sand pails for a child they no longer had. They worked out how this baby in the cart was a thing to take like any other, how the baby's mother, looking cold and prim and much too young, would recover soon enough. Later on, they would not be able to explain their dislike of her, how their plan to take a baby suddenly became a rescue mission in the span of three seconds, and yet it did. Their hearts pounded. This was the one, the very baby they were meant to pluck. She was meant for them.

Taking a baby, however, was supposed to be difficult, if not impossible. Nicholas figured it would go wrong with the simple act of reaching for her, that the gesture would tangle with all manner of botches, alarms and crashing gates. They would be caught even before they had made it ten feet. He looked at Audrey as she watched the baby, her eyes big and staring, her purple purse tucked under her arm, fat as a heart. She had stopped bathing recently, and though he had asked her to shower that morning, she was superstitious and wanted to continue her five-day hiatus, like a footballer before a big game. Her fear-soaked scent wafted around them, mixed with leatherette, polyurethane, artificial jasmine.

They weren't properly dressed for this, they were hardly altered. Nicholas had slicked back his hair, donned an old coat he could ditch, and Audrey had tucked her long hair under with pins, so she appeared to have a bob. Anybody who knew them even slightly, however, would be able to identify his large-nosed profile or her bumpy walk in a dark video ten seconds long. Anybody who could judge the situation would judge that they wanted to be caught. Still, hardly anybody knew them, and this was a day when white birds flocked. A fire door was left open two inches by employees sneaking smokes during their break, a toilet overflowed and dripped down to the basement electrical panel, and the surveillance system, never properly installed in the first place, was defective. All eyes, even the electronic ones, were either turned away or couldn't be relied upon. Nothing was true. With no wit among the witnesses, there was little to parse.

Still, the witnesses, such as they were, would argue for a full twenty minutes over who, exactly, had a red handbag, who looked at the chlorine bleach too long. None of which was known to Nicholas, who had had somewhat washy luck all his life; to him, he and Audrey were fluorescent, shifty, and left a trail of scent. They would be stopped before it got out of hand. He counted on it.

What he didn't count on was the baby's mother, that she would act in such alignment with their plan, slipshod as it was, that it wouldn't falter. The mother went to the next aisle, leaving the baby in the cart, fat and sweet and swiping her neck. Soft pretzels churned in the guts of the people watching the giant TVs, the toilet overflowed in the men's, and Margaux didn't miss a beat. She was the lunatic on aisle twelve where the mother happened to step. Margaux feigned confusion so expertly that the mother, after glaring at her for a full seventeen seconds, decided that maybe she was someone who needed help. The mother, absorbed in Margaux's neediness and inexplicable looks, said, "Can I get someone for you?" Margaux seemed familiar somehow, both gorgeous and wretched, like a misbehaving celebrity, and her hair seemed askew—which it was, being a cheap blonde wig snatched from the spot not far from the DVDs and the personal lubricants—and her eyes, enlarged by a pair of 2.5 reading glasses, also snatched, had a slight craziness to them. The mother, being barely nineteen and therefore undaunted by celebrity or craziness, tilted her head at Margaux and asked her again, "Is there someone I can get?" even as her baby was being carried off. Margaux let a pool of saliva shine on her lip and crossed her legs like she had to pee, suddenly bending down so that the mother gave a little surprised cry and reached out to touch Margaux's jacket (aisle four).

The baby felt electric to Nicholas, the twenty-four pounds and five ounces of her, as he pulled her from the cart. Her chubby legs curled up like a hedgehog, and she shoved a fist in her mouth. He felt her breathing, and what he believed was her soul—he believed deeply in souls, if not necessarily gods. He felt her gaze rocket through him, a hole through his chest. She had seemed tiny at first, but swelled in his clutch. The crisp dress and hot abdomen. Rather than run straight from the store, he luxuriated in these seconds of total awareness—what his Buddhist coworker and archnemesis at the accounting firm might call presence. Presence was never so grand, or fraught, or awful. But Audrey, panting, grabbed the baby. Her fingers scraped his, and the baby—this is when he really saw the lump and then suppressed the noticing—was gone from his hands. In a blink, Audrey placed the baby on her hip like an expert mother, like the mother of many children, though she had only had the one. It all came back, the nub of her hip as if meant for resting a baby, a feeling of terrible rightness.

This was all taking too long, they were dawdling. They should have been out the door by now. She shut her eyes, inhaled with a smile Nicholas hadn't seen in years, and it was on. They raced a few steps before catching themselves and lurched by the registers and through the glass doors that read *Entrance*—no matter, nobody noticed, not even the greeter who was digging in a pocket for the camping knife she wasn't allowed to have—and the alarms were quiet and the vestibule strangely devoid of people. They reached the parking lot and the baby swiveled her head, and Audrey's knees were about to buckle. Nicholas pressed his hand into her lower back and she would have felt it, except that she was numb.

Margaux wasn't far behind. She knew exactly when to calmly straighten up and smirk at the mother, who at last remembered the baby. By the time the mother was back to her empty cart and frantic, Margaux was on her way to the hair section to replace the wig and jacket, take a different pair of thick-framed glasses and a scarf. She wasn't even surprised to see the propped-open fire door right before she sailed through it, alarmless and unimpeded. She had, all her life, the expectation of hidden exits, money in the sofa crack, cabs waiting at the curb. She had a hard face that no one could pin down, she could change her bangs and her own mother would find her unrecognizable. Later on, she would show Nicholas how she had looked, laughing and flicking the glasses on and off her face like a deranged librarian. She would even imitate the mother's scream and Audrey hated that, especially if someone in another room could hear it, would have told her to shut up if Margaux hadn't helped them get the baby in the first place. Audrey paced the motel room with the baby and held her tight to her chest, and Nicholas said, "Careful. You want the baby to breathe, don't you?"

————————

His focus was clouded briefly by a delicious oblivion—which wasn't new but a thing since childhood when he had been incorrectly thought to be narcoleptic. He splashed water on his face in the motel bathroom and in the mirror was an astonishing vision, the face of a man getting away with something. Yet his surroundings were not ideal, were sodden in a way, as the motel stood on the side of the mountain range that scraped all the rain from the clouds, so the beds were damp and a ghost Hawaii stained the bathroom ceiling. He brought out the plastic cups in cellophane from the vanity, intending to pour drinks for him and Margaux. Audrey hadn't had a drink in two years, not since her last binge after Theodore. The baby was lodged on her hip as she paced. The moment of his victory was gone and he understood, as he surveyed their luggage and bags of food and diapers, their fugitive sprawl, that they were all fucked. Wildly fucked.

"What do you suppose her name is?" Margaux said, running her fingers over the baby's soft head until Audrey turned the baby away. "Well, she's a beautiful baby, even with the lump. I like her dress." Winked at her. "Expensive."

Audrey watched Nicholas over the top of the baby's head. "They'll be going over the tapes by now, wondering who are these assholes?" She cracked a tiny smile before her face was serious again. Nicholas saw a resemblance between her and the baby, identical slate eyes and doleful expressions. But the baby's gaze, as she moved in the arc that Audrey traced, stayed fixed on him. She didn't seem to blink.

"What's the lump about, do you suppose?" Margaux had taken the cups and was picking off the cellophane. It was an obvious thing to wonder, and yet he didn't want to invite the answer. Out in the world, buildings were dynamited, wars were underway, people drove their cars into rivers, sometimes on purpose, but it was in this place, this room, where he imagined chaos was about to wake. They were merely acting as if calm, as if the edge on which they were poised was only imaginary.

The baby suddenly whimpered and swiped at her neck, then her ear. Margaux said, "Do you think it's hurting her? What if she needs a doctor?"

Audrey put her hand over the baby's face and glared. Nicholas wanted her to be good to Margaux, not only because Margaux had agreed to do this, but because she was the one who, when baby Theodore died, sat with Audrey for days, lighting her cigarettes and pouring her vodka. Margaux was the one who had said that, since they couldn't afford more *in vitro*, perhaps they should consider other options and that she would help. She had a way of seeming she could conjure. She laughingly skipped straight over adoption and went to stealing. The awfulness of what she meant and their understanding of it, especially when they sobered up, seemed not to come from them, or not the selves they knew at least, but from an entitled logic sprung from loss. Theodore's death, senseless as any other because he had simply stopped breathing—and whether he had been wrapped or snuggled too tightly was undetermined—left not a void but a territory whose possibilities included everything but bringing him back. Nicholas had seen things he never thought he would see, and he watched Margaux then, how she stood, drunk and even vulnerable as she offered herself, in the wild's epicenter, and he found himself marveling at the creature who seemed to be his own discovery.

———————

The lump. The interior of which he assumed to be rife with infection but he couldn't be sure. The baby continued to stare at him, unsmiling. "Maybe it's just a swollen gland," he said.

Audrey pressed her lips to the baby's hair. "Maybe she's supposed to take medicine." The baby batted her neck and Audrey started hushing and jiggling her again.

Margaux picked up her jacket from one of the beds. "I'm going home now. Gotta feed the dog. See you tomorrow." Fluttered her fingers in the air and the door latched loudly behind her, and it seemed impossible, this coming and going, how unafraid she was. Impossible that he and Audrey should be left there, nestled in the motel's orange hues, sunset and rust and Fanta, with a baby who wasn't theirs stuffing her fingers in her mouth and continuing to stare at him. Fraudulent him. The baby understood him, how wrapped in doom. Her gaze said very serious things about this situation, that she was not to be owned. She softened a biscuit with her gums before shoving the whole thing in her mouth without once taking her eyes off him.

He took a valium secretly in the bathroom and all three of them slept until dawn, not as if they were comfortable, but as if, he thought, to escape each other. Audrey had left the nubby curtains slightly parted, so that in the morning a thin sun illuminated the baby. Nicholas could see as he watched her sleeping that the lump had something like a pimple on it. When Audrey woke, she sat up, stroked the baby's cheek, then carefully slid off the bed. Her breasts swung heavily under her T-shirt and Nicholas wondered if they were bigger, as if in metamorphosis—as if she could be pseudo-lactating. He had heard such a thing could happen, the mind could manifest amazing configurations. Thoughts were things. Look at what his own mind had allowed. His Buddhist coworker would secretly love, he felt, to see him in this room—

"Look after her, Nic!" she whispered, but her eyes were wild and her hair clung to her cheeks. She went to her purse and pulled out her rosary, then disappeared into the bathroom. There was hardly a morning that she didn't pray. He deserved, he knew, her rebuke; since they had entered the motel room he had barely touched the baby, hadn't even changed her diaper. He couldn't stand to recall the heavy feel of her when he pulled her from the cart, how overtaken by love he had been. He was amazed that she was sleeping now, and he allowed himself to think for a moment that maybe she trusted them.

He opened the door when Margaux rapped on it and saw his reflection in her enormous sunglasses. Her hair was still wet from the shower and dripped on the paper bag of bagels and hash browns she carried. He felt the pull of her as she sidled past.

"They don't know what the lump is." She stood cradling the bag as she watched the baby in the playpen. "I turned on the news—I had to. I know you said it was a bad idea, but I couldn't help it. The parents were on—"

"The parents—" He started blinking too much. He had hoped that the mother was alone, a teenage pregnancy or some such.

She removed her sunglasses. "The police chief said they don't know what the lump is and that the baby was supposed to see a doctor."

Nicholas took the bag from her arms and tried to focus on it, the feel of the paper and the smell of the hash browns, but the ordinariness was painful. "What the fuck have we done? How is this even possible?"

Margaux snorted. "All they have is six seconds of you and Audrey and the baby, and it's like yeti footage, completely blurry and useless. I could barely recognize you. So that's good news, Nic. Good news." She stepped close to him, took a bagel from the bag, ripped a piece off with her teeth. Without swallowing she said, "Want to know her name?"

"I already do," he said. "It's Thea."

On the third day, Thea's lump had something sticking out of it. Nicholas, Audrey, and Margaux stood around her, staring. The bit protruding was pure white and small, like a thorn or the end of a quill. Sometimes the baby cried and swiped at it, and other times she seemed to forget it was there. Her appetite was normal and she ate orange slices and jarred baby food, and she drank formula, bottle after bottle, which they warmed under the faucet. She crawled around on the floor, even played with the toys they had brought for her, and used the side of the bedspread to haul herself up to standing. She didn't laugh, but she didn't cry much either, and Nicholas could almost pretend that she was relatively content, except when she turned her gaze on him, her open stare pitiless and royal.

They left the motel room for a drive. Margaux sat in the front seat wearing a new wig and Audrey sat in the back with a baseball cap on, sobbing into her hands. Back in the motel, Nicholas had wrapped his arms around her, felt her shoulders jerking in a way he hadn't felt since Theo's funeral. She had shrugged him off, saying in a choked voice, "We're terrible people."

The baby now sat beside her in the car seat and Nicholas could feel Thea staring into the back of his head. He was aware, too, of other things, the pedestrians who were free, the inviting spaces beyond the minimarts and auto shops. Margaux's legs beside him. His brain, he felt, had been altered. He and Audrey had no plan from here. What, really, was the probability of what they had done in the first place, and what was the probability of getting away with it?

Margaux was turned around in her seat, saying what a beautiful baby Thea was, which was true enough, and she played with the little foot in the pink sock. For a moment, Nicholas imagined that the baby was smiling at her, but when he looked in the rearview mirror, Thea's eyes met his and her face was grim.

Audrey said, "Stop the car. I'm going to be sick."

Two hours later, it was Margaux who went to the trunk of the car in the rain and searched around in the toolbox after Nicholas said to get the needle-nose pliers. He and Audrey were looking at Thea's neck, at the half-inch of white string, or whatever it was, that poked out.

"Jesus, this is getting so weird." Margaux handed him the pliers and they all looked at each other. Nicholas remembered a rusted bent nail that his father had yanked from the bottom of his five-year-old foot, the shock of the bloodless, unburied tip. "Well, are you gonna do it?"

Audrey held up her hand, "Wait." Before Theo and the numerous miscarriages, before fertility drugs and *in vitro*, she had been a nurse, and a good one. She knew it should fall to her to extract whatever that was, but she simply couldn't manage it. With Thea on her hip gnawing a rubber ring, she pulled a disinfecting wipe from her purse and smoothed it over the lump. "Now, she's ready."

Margaux's eyes were big. "What if it hurts her when you pull?"

"Just do it," Audrey said, looking away as she held the baby up. The rubber ring bounced on the floor when Thea folded up her chubby legs and clutched her toes.

Nicholas fixed the pliers on the end of the little white protrusion. "This won't hurt, Thea, it's okay." He realized that it was the first time he had called her by her name. He tugged, gently, a millimeter at a time and the white piece emerged, one inch, two inches. Then it was free, a damp stick, and Thea's face hardly changed.

"It's a fucking feather," Margaux laughed. Audrey, her face pale and startled, carried the baby over to the bed and sat down with her. She kissed the top of her head.

Nicholas stood, holding the feather, unbelieving. Margaux turned her face to him and in the motel light he thought she seemed a little ravenous, maybe ecstatic. They all seemed to want something, to be caught in unending cycles of desire, or perhaps he misread her. She grinned and said, "She's a miracle baby, that one," and touched his hand.

During the episodes of his childhood, when he would involuntarily pass out for hours at a time, he sometimes had dreams. They were usually about white birds in various guises, the names of which came from the lists his birding father kept pinned to the fridge. The dream birds, once generic, morphed over the years to include pelicans, egrets, kites, snowy plovers and snowy owls, sanderlings and terns. On this night as he dreamed in the motel, it was mute swans that came, falling from the sky with their wings braking and feet outstretched, clouds of doves, and an albatross with a white body and grey wings, what his father could have told him was a mollymawk. A foolish gull.

Margaux also made an appearance in the dream, her breasts, her thighs, forms that rose to the surface and descended again and caused a rush of arousal so strong that it woke him. After a while, he watched the wooliness of the dark room, the furniture and the people in it. The feather was beside him on the nightstand, because none of them could throw it away. It seemed like something they could make a wish on and find themselves back in time before the baby. The heating unit grated noisily and took periodic rests. Thea slept in her playpen between the two beds. If he sat up slightly he could see the rise and fall of her chest, the balled fists. He hadn't known a baby who could sleep so well, who could impose so little upon the adults, and yet he hadn't known anyone so imperious. The baby of the shopping cart was, in reality, a ruler. Anyone who could sprout a feather from her neck was the one in control.

He assumed Audrey was next to him, but his adjusting eyes

saw the figures in the other bed. It took him a moment to remember that Margaux had decided to stay the night with them, that she and Audrey had been huddled at the door around 9 p.m., and that Margaux, who had been holding her purse and jacket, had stepped back into the room and put down her things.

The figures in the bed murmured to each other, and a realization spread over Nicholas as he watched them that what he was seeing was a single entity. Margaux's fingers with their metallic nail polish clutched the sides of Audrey's face like talons, or that's what he would have sworn to, except that what he saw in the shifting of his wife's body, and he immediately recognized it, was her response to pleasure. The two forms were seeking each other out, the mouths touching together almost with a magnetic click. He closed his eyes, felt himself sink back under the weight of the double valium he had ingested right before bed.

In the morning when he woke at last, the feather remained, but Audrey, Margaux, and the baby were gone. The playpen sat empty like a drained pond, with a pacifier and flannel blanket pooled at its center. On a piece of paper on the bureau, with the motel pen beside it, nothing floated except for his name written hastily and abandoned, and near the door there was a small jumble of clothes they had decided to leave without.

Sometimes, he knew, it is best to stay very, very still, and so it was two hours before he got up, raked his hair, swallowed some tap water. He saw that they had left him some bread and saltines, peanut butter and a large bag of trail mix. Half a can of formula. What to do was intangible, how to touch his feet to the outside world seemed impossible. It was better to think, instead, of the room as his and simply settle in, do what he and Audrey had always done, which was wait. Waiting could be almost professional, if the mind was trained on it. Seconds could fall open like canyons.

He waited for two days, sometimes watching the feather or the callouses on his feet, or pressing salt grains into his fingertips. He spoke out loud and the sound of it seemed too much, as did the toilet flushing and the ringing phone in the next room, so when the banging on his door finally began, it was a blow to his ribs, his sternum. They called his name and banged the door, and he stood on the other side of it, looking at the instructions, which had been glued at an angle, for what to do in case of a fire. They continued banging, and he went back to the bed and sat down on it. He picked up the feather and turned it in his fingers before placing it in his mouth. He put his head on the pillow and considered the feather, how familiar it was, because it was soft and also sharp.

The reader has now a repertoire of poisonous and harmless preparations
from which he may choose. As for myself . . . I pin my faith to formula
No. 4, viz., my Preservative Soap for the inside of the skin, and a wash
of benzoline or turpentine liberally applied from time to time—say
twice a year—to the outside of all uncased or exposed specimens.

—MONTAGU BROWNE, *PRACTICAL TAXIDERMY*

APPETITES

The wolves patrol back and forth and back and forth along the forest periphery and terrify the village children but not the parents— the parents are too busy with their politics and knickknacks to notice much about the wolves. They send the children out each day into the playgrounds and streets and forests with nothing but a hush-hush, and so the children, with their dirt-lodged nails and smudged cheeks, become feral by daylight and try not to lose their holey mittens or stray alone too close to the woods. The wolves do not often succeed in making a catch because the children are streetwise and aggressive and carry pocketknives or pieces of glass or even nunchakus (if someone had bothered to query a wolf, in fact, he would say that the preferred comestible would be an ungulate or a stoat), though occasionally a score is rumored to be had. Armed or otherwise, no child has been able to kill a wolf. The book was written so that a child is eaten or will occasionally outsmart her lupine stalker, or a child is lifted out from the guts of a wolf by her woodsman-rescuer, but a child never takes her nunchukas and beats the daylights out of the wolf.

II

Against the wishes of her parents, Red considers herself a pacifist and doesn't even carry a pocketknife. Once, she strangled a vole but she had been very young and couldn't provide an explanation for it now. She has not expected to be in peril for her life because she suspects the wolves are just misunderstood, until the day a scrubby boy named Jake removes a small book from his jacket and says, "You might want to read this." She takes the book from him cautiously; she knows that he recently pulled the whiskers from a cat and she can smell him from where she stands. When she peruses the book, she sees the forest path, the grandmother's end—and the wolf, how he lies in wait for the hooded girl. There are implications, too, that the girl will undress herself and get into bed with the wolf. There are implications that she is complicit in her own devouring. Jake is patient while Red reads and, when she closes the book, says, "Don't you have to walk through the forest to get to your grandma's?"

Because she is a girl of few words, Red says nothing and Jake smirks at her and licks his fingertips, slides away on his skateboard. She looks again at the girl in the ruby cloak and the girl looks very much like Red. (Red doesn't own anything crimson or vermillion or even brick. Nor does she have auburn hair, or a hot temper, and she is only just awakening to her name's incongruity.) The drawings inside the book are finely done, but Red is disturbed by the consumptive depiction of the wolf, as if he has been hungry for many years, and the way the girl's cheeks are flushed. More so with each passing illustration. Grandmother, too, disturbs her because she is rendered in the palest watercolors, as though fading away even before the wolf can disembowel her.

|||

Red's grandmother lives in an institution on the far side of the forest where all the people go who have started forgetting. She first forgot her house keys in various places, then she forgot the words for presumptuous and katydid, and then the name of her cat. Then she forgot her husband and was taken to the institution in a wagon lined with the silver fur of wolves. Red's grandfather visits his wife on Sundays and brings her vinyl recordings of songs from their youth, which she appears to occasionally remember. Sometimes she recognizes Red but often she doesn't, and Red will put the bottle of wine or loaf of bread or custard that she has brought for her on a side table and then, settling into a chair beside her grandmother's bed, and despite being a girl of few words, begins to tell her a story. Sometimes Grandmother looks up and smiles into the space around Red's brown hair.

IV

The forest is full of snowy hemlocks, and sugar maples, and, in warmer seasons, ferns. The children collect the young fiddleheads in spring, roast them with butter on small fires they build inside old metal drums or pits in the ground. They eat ants dipped in bottled chocolate sauce, periwinkles gathered from the shore and pulled from their shells with straight pins, and sometimes, on a dare, they eat the soil from the forest path. In winter, they smoke tobacco, stolen from their parents and laced with spices, and they make their own moonshine out of plums and nail polish, serving it to each other in tiny paper cups; no one drinks it, however, no one takes the dare. No one, that is, except for Jake. And this explains a good deal.

V

A wolf sees Red from a distance, sees her riding her scooter along the plowed concrete path at the edge of the hemlocks. She is somewhat large compared to his usual deer pâté and crackers but she also appears delectable as he has been without a catch for many days. He has tried eating broccoli with balsamic glaze, and potatoes with rosemary, and scrambled eggs with a dusting of wood ashes, and so he has said to his friends that he has tried, really tried, but it is not enough, and what he desires most is a girl who smells of meat and bleeds once a month and has small hills of flesh starting to form on her chest. "I need my meat," he says and his friends nod, without irony.

There is another wolf who overhears this conversation. He nearly chokes on his latté. Wolves like that asshole, he thinks, give wolves a bad name. Wolves like him are the reason that his kind are feared the world over, and for little reason. How many humans can you name who have been killed by a wolf? "Exactly the point!" he says out loud, and all the wolves turn and look at him before he skulks away, muttering.

VI

The cloak is missing. The cloak of blood or pomegranates or rage, the cloak woven in wool with a small gold clasp and a languid hood. The cloak of cloaks, and not one that hides the wearer but one that marks, like a fawn bleeding out on snow or a thought you don't want to think. The cloak of no pockets and nothing inside but the child's small body, the cloak that ripples out at the edges when the wind catches it, the cloak with a cold silk lining. The cloak is missing, and it is missing not because Red has misplaced it or buried it in the clay banks of the river but because it was not given to her in the first place. The grandmother made the cloak of no pockets after she forgot the word for impractical and before the last time she spoke her husband's name. Thereafter the cloak was one of forgetting and she has no recollection of carefully ironing the seams before she sewed them shut, no memory of choosing and fixing the gold clasp. No memory at all. If a cloak goes missing in a forest and no one remembers it, does the cloak actually exist?

VII

Jake, high on moonshine and mud cakes sprinkled with smoked rabbit feces, follows Red where she scoots along the path. She stops intermittently to admire the winterberries against the snowy banks or the trees whose leaves still hang like bronze ornaments. She mentally composes a song whose notes she picks based on a calculus equation she is working out in school, and reviews what she learned at the library while researching glossolalia in the time of ancient Byblos. Hearing the occasional crunch of Jake's feet on the snow, she makes sure not to alert him by hurrying and she stares straight ahead.

After a while, silence coasts in like an enormous dark bird and the crunch on the snow is no more. Red halts her scooter and looks behind her. The snowy village lies in the distance and she realizes how far she's travelled. When she turns around again, Jake is standing in her path with the bottom of his foot pressed against the scooter's wheel.

"Hullo, Red." The top of his turtleneck sweater is rime-coated where it rests against his salivating mouth. The skin of his frigid hands is broken and bleeding. He grins and Red shivers. "Wolf got your tongue?"

Red is staring down at his raw hands, her eyes wide.

Because he knows how this goes, he growls, "All the better for abducting you." As if from nowhere, a knife in his grasp. "Tut-tut, Red. You should always be prepared for the worst."

She produces from her jacket the book he'd given her, almost prompting a slash from the knife, but he pauses, and, there, in the moment of his hesitation lies her succor. Tossing the book to the sidewalk, she says, "I have spells, motherfucker," and pronounces some words she knows, the strange ones from ancient Byblos, until Jake is dazzled. There is a popping sound, then a fizz, and he turns, as tidy as that, into a loaf of bread. Red suppresses the urge to stomp the loaf and picks it up instead, tucks it under her arm where she feels its steaminess.

Hearing the not-so-distant howling of wolves, she pushes off hard on her scooter and heads straight for her grandmother, the pack snorting and huffing somewhere behind her all the way.

VIII

The building where Red's grandmother lives has a lobby with a fireplace, overstuffed chairs with wolf throws, and a coffeemaker. Beyond the lobby, the building smells of chemicals and the walls are covered in white tiles. Her grandmother sits in a room at the end of a long corridor and if she remembers that she has forgotten, then she will try to remember, but if she has forgotten forgetting then she stares at the painting of hemlocks that hangs on her wall and is captivated by its mystery.

As the scooter races over the sidewalks, Red can hear the wolves clamoring nearer. Their rasping breath and meaty, musky scent means they are almost upon her when she hurls the Jake-loaf, still hot, through the twilit air. The first wolf who seizes it is the latté-drinking one—the big faker!—and then the others bite him hard as punishment before they grab the loaf themselves and rip it to shreds. Pronouncing it the most delicious morsel they've ever tasted—stinky with sweat and moonshine and essence of rabbit—they resolve to eat bread more often, though they will find it is never quite the same.

Red has long since left her scooter in the lobby and reached the doorway of her grandmother's room. Grandmother watches the painting of hemlocks from the edge of her bed, her spine in silhouette a spindly arc under her cardigan, her small bony feet inside a pair of wolf slippers.

Red is overcome with love for her. "I'm so sorry, Grandmother. I had a loaf of bread for you, but it wasn't good enough."

Grandmother turns her face toward the voice and Red can see: two clear eyes. "I had a cloak for you, my dear . . . Never mind. Perhaps it never was. Come sit with me and look at the hemlocks."

Red sits on the bed beside her grandmother as the sound of the wolves' howls swells and fades into nothing, until the wolves themselves disappear, and the murmurs and wails of the institution, the tile walls and chemicals, dissolve, and nothingness flows around Red like a terrible and lovely sea until she is left with only the wind nudging the very tips of the forest trees, which are barely there, and Grandmother's faint breathing.

Plate IV.

LION MOUNTED FROM THE "FLAT."

*Should it be wished to open the mouth to express rage
or what not, the edges of the skin of the mouth, being
no doubt destitute (in a "flat" skin) of their inner lining
(the mucous membrane), must have this replaced.*

—MONTAGU BROWNE, *PRACTICAL TAXIDERMY*

PHONE BOOTH

*The problem with missing people is the charge they leave in the at-*mosphere. It short-circuits everything, and the crackling spaces are almost deafening. Salsman and I have an ongoing argument about them, the Missing. He is reading a book while I click the television remote and bathe in the flickering blue of strangers who aren't with us anymore. People get into cars or planes, go through doors, go for walks, appear momentarily at shopping malls or crowded fairs and never again. No one actually sees them go. They peel off from the Earth, from the ones they love, from the ones they don't, and there are so many of them that the news outlets can't keep up. No one reads the names anymore.

The skeptics, and Salsman is one, say that people have always vanished and there is only a greater tendency to notice the absences. He is solidly in his chair, he points out, his molecules perfectly aligned into a tangible, animate substance. He pats his stomach and says he is even more here than usual.

I know a woman who claimed that she got out of her car in the dawn light, after her shift at the hospital, and noticed something move around the corner of her house. It was her elderly mother, which should have been impossible, she said, because her mother was wheelchair bound. This version of her mother walked around the corner of the house and was never seen again. The police have stopped investigating, and the woman's own daughter said, "She was just old, Ma. Just old."

Salsman says to me, "You're an eccentric noticing other eccentrics. You just don't like them impinging on your territory."

If Salsman doesn't believe in the Missing, he does like to entertain notions of the end. "The missing people, the idea of them," he says, "is only a conceptual shift. We went from hysterical, incendiary versions of the End Times to more nuanced ones. Now it's absence as opposed to death." He closes his book and smiles. "Piecemeal annihilations."

There is no one stopping this ending, it seems. It strikes me that part of the problem is the lack of a money shot, since the actual moment of vanishing goes unrecorded. There is only the past tense, the photos of people, some already blurry in their daily lives, collected from the families and showing them as they were. In many cases, there is video footage of the last time they were seen, at least by an electronic eye, which is played on a loop, so you see a man, for instance, walk along a subway platform, reach the end and begin again. This becomes the most important thing about him, apart from the fact that he is missing.

———

Salsman and I take a trip to the desert because he is tired of water and feels it is time to dry out. He brings the bourbon along anyway. He is a retired analyst and, above everything, too old for me. I fought it for as long as I could, had webby, sulfurous dreams about filling prescriptions for blue pills and the rubbing of arthritic feet, but one day when I laid out my arguments, he simply stopped trying to uncork the twenty-five-year-old scotch whose time he felt was up and said, "None of that will matter. It's not like any of us will get really and truly old." It is possible that he was toying with me; humor assembles in my brain like a Picasso portrait, and so I smile, or don't, at the wrong spots sometimes. Even occasionally sob on the tail end of a big laugh. Salsman, being Salsman, considers this evidence of our compatibility.

We are driving along quiet, open roads and he is expounding. "We should all be having a better time, if you think about it. Nobody truly believes they're going to die—nobody—but virtually everybody masturbates their worries to death. And god knows—and that's god with a small *g*—that that endless stroking gave me an entire career, but still. It does get gloomy." He says this mock-gloomily and does something strange with his face. We are in his car, which he has neglected so badly that it is stripped down and corroded to the point of imminent disintegration. He says he keeps driving it because he likes the conceptual rhyme of being one hollowed-out shell riding inside another. This is the kind of thing that he thinks is funny. I am the one driving, though, my fingers curled around the steering wheel, which is peeling.

Salsman digs into the glove box, finds a bottle, and pours bourbon into his plastic mug as the scene outside the car grows drier and paler. There are low mountains in the distance that look like a stack of books that were dropped in water and left to puff up in the sun. "You can't do that," I say, and grab the cup from him, empty it out my window and hand it back. The secret is that he likes being maneuvered, if only briefly. He pretends to drink from the mug.

"Okay, consider yesterday," he says, "the news story about the old woman—ninety something. She wakes up in Florida with a kinkajou sitting on her chest and caressing her face. A kinkajou! Caressing her face! Imagine how long it's been since somebody has done that." He strokes his chin. The road seems eternal, slithery. "So, she screams, then it screams. It takes off for the attic, where, it turns out, it's been camped, eating the oranges it was stealing from her kitchen." He takes a pen and tiny notebook from his shirt pocket and writes something, but I can't see what it is. "It's sort of miraculous, don't you think? It's like Fuseli's *The Nightmare*, but better. Live action. What do you suppose the kinkajou wanted?"

"I don't know, Salsman. I don't know."

We stop at a gas station and he goes inside the store to buy carrot juice and medjool dates, anything virtuous he says. I get out to fill the tank and when I pull the nozzle from the pump, I notice the sticker on it, close to the handle: *Improper Use May Cause a Hazardous Condition*. This is the problem with the end of things, you start to read every scrabble of words for code. As the numbers on the gas gauge tick away, I watch a coyote dart behind the gas station and reappear across the road. The sky is expanding, filling its pink lungs. It is six o'clock in the morning. Salsman comes out of the minimart with a paper bag and smoking a cigarette. "See that?" he says, spreading his arms. "We're the only people alive."

———————

Which isn't even metaphorically true. As he loves to point out to the panickers, the numbers are still the same. People believe, he says, that the population has been decimated because it is more exciting to believe than not; all you have to do is haul up the census data to see that everything is more or less the status quo. "People have gone missing," he says, "since we were pulling each other's hair in the caves. It's what we do. People go missing."

———————

He was not only an analyst, but mine. I cradled my addled mind in layers of identity: I was Sola, I was Serafina in socks, I was Shoshanna on the dotted line, I was Sylvia Plath. It worked, his listening skills, his attentions, or time did it. I wasn't the only patient to get a little better. A few of us started to want a kind of lucidity, to lacerate the medicated veil in front of our eyes. I convinced Salsman to stop my Thorazine and set me free. I felt a sudden puritan jonesing for clarity. I set fire to his diagnostic manual, having packed the rips and shreds of it inside a metal trashcan on his back porch, and he didn't stop me. He stood there watching me and watching the small flames pop from the rim. He told me once about the male primal urge to douse fire with a spray of urine—a classic example of the ideas with which he is sometimes afflicted—but he just kept his hands in the pockets of his old khakis, his shirtsleeves rolled up to the elbows. (He has incongruously muscular arms and I sometimes call him Popeye, which, he pointed out to me, constitutes a joke, if not a good one.)

"You surpass fire," was all he said.

Sometimes the road unravels in slight curves. There are alternating flats and hills, tufts of shrubs. Everything seems to be far away, and gummy pools of light swallow the occasional distant car ahead of us. I wonder if Salsman sees this as I do. The missing people bend light, they bend air. As I breathe, molecules of absence flutter in. Lung Moths. Lepidoptera dust on the exhale, a person passing through.

Salsman says he's hungry, and I say, "The convenience store already presented itself. Hours ago."

"The diner will present itself, my dear, because it always does," and not twenty minutes later, bright as laundry on a line, a diner on the roadside. It takes us another five minutes to reach it and Salsman suggests I'm driving too slowly, but I'm not. There are eight cars in the parking lot, which seems ample considering the space that has been washing around us. You wonder where they came from. Time is starting to make me ache, and distance. Part of a small flying saucer is attached to the side of the building.

Salsman waves at the waitress and selects two stools for us at the counter. He detests the confining nature of booths. There are two televisions showing the news where names of the Missing scroll along the bottom, but the anchor is talking about something else entirely. The waitress doesn't write down our order. She listens while staring at our faces and I wonder if she's using some kind of memory device to keep everything straight, if we are wearing hash-brown hats and lemons dangle from our ears. Perhaps she is even making an attempt at mind reading. Salsman says that apple pie is utterly humorless, so he opts for the lemon meringue. She winks at me before leaving.

"I have to wash my hands," I say. I remember hearing that if you are feeling guilty about something you should wash your hands.

Salsman is checking his phone, but there is still no service. "Oh, I don't think you want to use the washrooms here." He laughs.

I glance down at my hands, how surreal they feel, unattached to me. Somehow I have caused it, the missing people, the missingness. Salsman is half turned on the stool, watching me, and I can smell him and want to curl up in his lap, a cat or child. The ache makes my body ring.

I realize minutes, maybe, have come and gone when he says, "Where'd you go off to?"

"I don't know."

He says this is an existential diner. "People just don't understand the apocalypse. They don't get how it works. They think it's one thing, when it's another." I think he says apocalypse, but maybe it was eclipse. Or lisp. Or appalling lapse.

The waitress brings plates of beef stroganoff, toast, and hash browns. The parsley sprigs are overly green, a leprechaun in the visual cortex.

"Bless you," Salsman says, as if he is a pious man. He has two children, but they no longer live with him. They are trekking in Mogadishu, Nairobi, Mombasa, Zanzibar. Or somewhere. A kind of missingness, but Salsman doesn't mind. It is okay to love them this way, they say, from afar. Salsman says they are growing up.

"Maybe I shouldn't be here," I say. "I have stories to file."

"You don't have stories to file. You're not a journalist."

I pick at the noodles, but I'm unable to eat. I am, however, an artist of the non sequitur, which is not so much a talent I cultivate as one that simply presents itself, implacable. Here's how it works: *Moby Dick* suddenly appears in my mind and so I say, "Melville." Salsman squints at me, waiting. I continue: "Ishmael gives a description of Captain Ahab—you remember? He describes him as a mute, maned sea lion."

Salsman still doesn't say anything, but *Moby Dick* is one of his favorite books and I have his full attention. Sometimes I think he would fuck my brain if he could. "The first time I read that sentence," I say, "all I saw was the word *lion*. I didn't realize that it was another kind of creature altogether that was being described. A near lion, but in the end not a real one."

"And?"

"You're not an exact lion. You're a line I misread."

Salsman clutches at his heart. A laugh rockets from my chest and various heads turn to see who the lunatic is. He can mock me openly now and it delights me. He has already seen every variation of spasmodic, shrieking human, he has seen us all in our pajamas and slippers, sweating as our demons boiled us, and therefore he is impossible to surprise or, moreover, shame. I have never seen embarrassment curdle his face. He is safe in his role of benevolent overseer, even now, and I am the freak I am. He grins and stuffs hash browns into his mouth.

After a while, I say, "The thing is, I think I'd like to go missing. I'd like to feel that. Wouldn't you? Don't you wonder what happens to them?"

Salsman is quiet while he butters his toast. Then: "Leah didn't go missing, sweet pea. She committed suicide. Remember?"

Which at one time would have been a grenade straight into my forehead, except now I'm only annoyed. Leah was my closest friend on the floor, fellow prisoner and addict of various pharmaceuticals and maladies. Bright as a new penny, hair like a stoplight. She singed my eyes, my brain. I know perfectly well that she wasn't a suicide, but one of the Missing. If I could spread the tangle of my thoughts on the surgery bed, perhaps I would find, among the sinuous horrors and what Salsman refers to as my father issues, strands of envy, even curiosity about her state. How she became a void. I didn't see her leave. What I saw was a black zippered body bag on a gurney being solemnly wheeled to the hyenic shrieks (only the everyday kind, nothing new) of a guy who spent his life in noise-blocking headphones and the head nurse who was having a fit that the body bag was being taken out in front of an audience of patients. I don't know what, or who, was actually in the bag. Leah pulled off something incredible and a vortex spins in her place.

"I remember," I say. There is one problem, though, with my theory of her disappearance. She shot a cold, terrible light, and her strength was legendary—it would take three orderlies, leather restraints, and a slug of Haloperidol to pin her down. My theory of the Missing is that they must be thin people, not thin physically, but psychically. They must be hardly there in the first place, they have to be faint people, so lifting them off to somewhere else is almost inevitable. Their electrons are loose and disconnected from each other, demagnetized. They are people, I figure, who are already part gone, and you couldn't say that about Leah.

Still, she is nowhere to be found.

There is a bend in the counter and I have a clear view of a large man sitting on one of the stools, his stomach touching the counter edge. He has an oily face, some stubble, and holding back the bit of long hair that remains on his head is a pink plastic barrette, shiny as aspirated bubble gum. The barrette is everything dissonant and perfect. It makes me ache even more than distance and time.

"You're tearing up," Salsman says. He squeezes a lemon slice on my hash browns, which is how I like them, and somehow I taste it, as if I have been opening my mouth for him, waiting to lick a pill from his fingers. Take away the pain, I think, but then what really is pain? Only an idea, he would say. To sit in the existential diner, feeling all the tiny flicks on my skin, is to be surrounded by tiny acidic ideas. *Quiet quiet*, I think. But Salsman can't hear me.

"There is no apocalypse," he says. "No missing people. Other than the usual kind." It seems that his declaration, its simplicity, is evidence of his concern for what he would call my mode. I can't help myself, however, or the paragraph, flat and desperate, that assembles itself right in my voice box and unfurls in a thin stream. It is not as if I can't hear myself; I know how I seem.

"The believers stake out government property, Salsman, they haul giant signs up the sides of buildings, dangle messages from skyscrapers. I've seen them. Prostitutes and drugs addicts, especially, are missing in droves. Politicians are afraid to attach themselves to a problem with no conceivable foundation or solution," I say, balling up my fists. "I must write about it. I have stories to file. The Paper is waiting."

Salsman peels open a sugar packet and shakes it into his coffee.

In spite of being the most unflappable of our overseers, the most compassionate, he was still booted out, disgraced, for that lowliest thing of all, love—and not just that, but the sexual kind. We are reduced to this, we humans. Even he has pointed to the wet spot on the bed sheet and proclaimed, "Mollusk of love," though he laughed about it. We are slime. And perhaps this is it: the ones who go missing are the drier variety, powdery, their water content already diminished for easier transport, easier liftoff. They employ a kind of hydraulics or it is inflicted upon them. This accounts for the lack of weight I have been theorizing, Leah's fiery quality. We are in the right location for this, Salsman and I, for drying out. But I hold out no hope for Salsman, who has wet, sparkling eyes and damp breathing. He is all fluidity, even at his age, and so it is up to me to discover what this is all about. The transmutation of molecules into absence, nothingness.

"How are you doing, darling?" is all he says. The Missing exert a pressure that I feel in my sinuses, screwing into my brain. All those nameless names, all the debris left behind. A kind of heat on my face, as if they burn up fuel as they go. Does he not feel it?

"I am well. Very well. Why do we say that, anyway, 'well'? People tumble into wells sometimes, get stuck. They are often full of water. People disappear into them. I am well."

Salsman makes some scratches in his notebook and looks at me, waiting for more. But I say nothing. Erasure at its usual pace. A pink barrette, a citrus bloom. Bright and sharp, in the mouth.

I tell him that I have to go to the bathroom, but instead I veer to the door and slip out, which is easy, only dust-mote travel on the entryway air stream. I figure I have five minutes, maybe ten, before he wonders what has happened, so I have to hustle along the bald eternal roadside to where there is a curve and a small sweet hill to obscure, hopefully, my vanishing point. I imagine that later he will note to the police or whomever that I am wearing the peach dress he got for me a few months ago when he was in a vintage store looking for a pair of boots already worn by somebody else. I am wearing peaches in the desert. I blend in to the dun. I hustle.

The interesting thing about the Missing is that very occasionally one of them is found, and they always seem to be gobsmacked, panting with the impossibility of going home. They rarely have anything useful to say about the experience and so they are deemed to be the usual cases of abduction. Perhaps I will have a different experience; I will come back with useful information. I will explain to Salsman the mystery he has been denying. I will file my story. I will have some concern over which name to pick as my byline, but nevertheless I will file (a joke!).

The temperature is not too warm at all. We have arrived at the right hour, though I could have a new set of problems with the setting sun. The desert is not emptiness exactly, but an accumulation of hidden things, and here and there the formation of dunes brought from the arid basins of what were once lakes, maybe, the sand brought on the wind, grain by grain and piled. The angle of repose. There are clutches of green spikes and frenzies: yuccas, cacti, creosote bushes. It occurs to me, suddenly, that since I am not walking this road in the searing heat and therefore the drying out is likely to be a slower process, I should prepare myself to be out here for a while. But I have no idea.

*   *   *

It is hard to say the passing of time, how much. Temporal elastics in the form of road, sand.

Up ahead, a lump on the pavement. Which turns out to be a large turtle, glacially crossing the road. I'm surprised at his size, which is not Galapagos, but heftier still than the usual desert box turtle. How bizarre at this juncture to have a companion, shell-bound. He lifts each foot with luxurious disregard for oncoming cars, except that there aren't any. Only the distant hum of a motorcycle. He drags himself like a struck knight pulling his body across the moors. He pauses, though, stops entirely on the painted line, and I don't like this, because it seems that I'm supposed to do something, and maybe this is part of the plan. I don't know how I'm going to hustle him off the pavement, since picking him up doesn't seem like something I want to do, but I keep walking up the side of the road.

Then I start to run a little, and I feel my sweat vanishing as if creatures are drinking it. Epidermis Lappers. Assistants, maybe. The turtle seems to be either ignoring the sound of the motorcycle or entranced by it. He is immutable on the centerline, but I still run and this must be how it goes, how it happens. Suddenly the motorcycle is there and going past me, the turtle like a leather clasp between the two open lanes. Even with emptiness all around, the motorcycle carves toward the line, right into the turtle, which is sent on a high arc, the heavy shell rotating underneath him 180 degrees, those wrinkled legs picking at the fast air. When he lands, he smashes like an egg, and the egg, as it turns out, contains eggs and he is not a he at all. The ruptured abdomen spills large white orbs as wet and unfortunate as a brain ruffling from a skull. The motorcycle drones away, smaller, fainter. Nothing nothing. Turn away from.

I keep walking and the road keeps unraveling.

The hit, I think, was aimed at me. And so I have made an error, maybe, I have misunderstood. A dislocation of location, a misalignment of longitude or latitude, I don't know which, or both, though this is to be expected—I am told I am terrible with directions. And this from Salsman, who still lets me drive his car, and who is to be trusted, and so I'm starting to think that maybe I should not have left him there.

I keep walking in the direction away from the diner, even with my doubts. The Missing are flicks and shadows around me, even though I can't make them out, even in sunlight. I take out my phone and peer at its smudged, dark face anyway. No service, which I already knew. The air is full of particles but not the communicating kind. The waves are not cellular and so I keep walking.

Then there is a post on the roadside, so far away. The getting there is endless and then the arrival, a kapow. You would think the lead-up would mitigate surprise. The bigger surprise still is that the post is big and wide and turns out to be a phone booth. Which is like seeing a polar bear, or a dodo.

The door folds together only partway before getting stuck, so I have to squeeze myself inside the booth. The bottom seems to be damp, despite the dryness of the air, but the moisture is maybe the remnant of some other Missing (perhaps people piss with fear when they are taken?), and maybe the ground material is deliquescent. We can only wonder the process.

Being inside the booth is like having an exoskeleton. The rings on my fingers rub against the metallic cord of the receiver and sound like crickets, like the jaws of mantises chewing. The phone is hard against my ear and warm, as if recently pressed to another head. There is no message I could give that would make sense. Even if I had some coins. Language inside the exoskeleton is all clicks and creaks. I have been, all along, a fluid creature, in the way of Salsman.

The door opens like wings sliding back, effortless this time, and I step out to see that the road is still there, still the same.

There is the distinct buzz and purr of a car. I know the sound even before I see the wrecked transport and Salsman with his hand waving out the window, a wondrous dust flying about the wheels. I feel the presence of the booth behind me, a past thing, a past. And I wonder if, when animals shed a skin, they look back to see themselves. Do they wonder at the shadow, armored and empty. Do they want it back?

part II

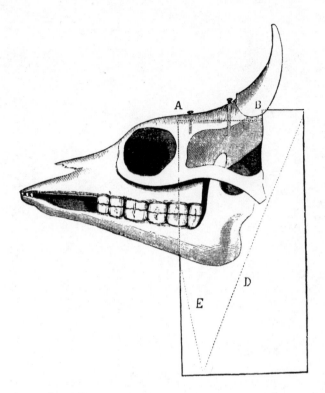

FIG. 26.—SKULL OF HORNED HEAD, BLOCKED READY FOR MOUNTING.

In this way the lamb flies from the wolf; thus the deer flies from the lion; thus the dove flies from the eagle with trembling wing; in this way each creature flies from its enemy: love is the cause of my following thee.

—OVID, *METAMORPHOSES*

AMBIVALENCE: A PROLOGUE

A writer was working on a story that troubled her. Her friend said that she should not write about Bluebeard, and he hated fairy tales. Why did writers keep coming at fairy tales like that, why not leave well enough alone? Write something else, for crying out loud! "Make something up," he said.

She continued to work at it anyway, over many months, when the sun was close and the lawns crisp. Winter came and she continued working on the story wearing sweaters and a long scarf. She thought perhaps she was cold not because there was snow outside, but because she was writing about a man who killed his wives. What she really wanted to write about was his last wife, number seven, and that meant a story in which six women existed merely as a mention, as corpses to be discovered.

She had to admit to herself that she wanted them to be slight, as she herself did not want to investigate the room where the bodies were kept or for the murders to ruin the life of the last remaining wife. For the months that she had been working on the story she'd become fond of the Seventh, even though her friend had snorted at her and told her to write about poverty or the war in Afghanistan. "Now that," he said, "is something to write about."

She returned to writing about the Seventh, and one night, as she discovered how a story can shift, seemingly organically, from being about one person to being about another—and in spite of knowing that her friend despised people who drank—she drank heavily. She consumed two brandies, three rum-and-diets, one and a half manhattans, two fingers of scotch, and a flute of champagne, and it affected her not a jot. Even her spelling remained impeccable and she noted the following morning that she had used *myriad* correctly. As in, there were myriad reasons to abandon the story.

The man brought her orange juice and French fries and pretended that he was unaware of the state of her apartment and the empty cocktail glasses beside the empty champagne flute. "Perhaps," he said, "you should write about the garbage island in the Pacific, or write about Syria. Yes, Syria. Now *that* is some Syri-ous shit . . ."

She grabbed the papers off her sofa before he nearly sat on

them. She said, "You can write about Syria if you want. In fact, why not go there?"

"Or the polar bears. Tell the people about them, the starving melting bastards." He was feeling warm himself and on the verge of sweating. He loved the woman, deeply, even if she didn't realize it. He had never been adept at this sort of thing and he could see that his offering of French fries and orange juice was being rejected. If only he had the offering she would accept, if only he had the right idea. She loved ideas! She was a woman of ideas. The NSA surveillance program maybe, or the Israeli-Palestinian conflict might move her. Surely there was one.

She had a distant look in her eye. "My mother," she said, "is very wise; she said something to me that I haven't forgotten."

"Never trust a man who does yoga?"

"Well, yes, she did say that. You have a good memory. But she also said: Never trust someone who doesn't swear."

Hope functions best in the presence of the ambiguous and so he was flooded with it. He opened the orange juice and took a healthy swig. He arranged some of the French fries on a paper napkin and began to munch them thoughtfully as he sat beside the woman.

To Imitate Blood—Frequently blood is required to be shown, as in instances where some animal may be represented tearing its prey. Usually this is done by thickly painting on vermilion and red lead mixed with varnish, or brushing on red lead mixed with thick glue, as a base on which to subsequently lay the vermilion. I may point out, however, that blood differs in tint, and the appearance of torn flesh, fresh blood, and coagulated blood is best got by painting the parts with wax, and tinting, with a little vermilion, some madder brown, or madder lake (a rather expensive color), and light red, arranged and blended one with the other as in nature.

—MONTAGU BROWNE, *PRACTICAL TAXIDERMY*

THE BASTARD NOTEBOOK

No one knows how old he is, but on his birthday he is surrounded by his captives and enablers and not one but three chocolate buttercream cakes. More to the point is that the beard has reached its apex, being more fulsome and deranged than ever, more blue. So don't imagine irony, or a placid sky or robin's egg. From twenty feet away, which is the closest a person would want to be, the color says poisonous creature or degraded food: don't lick or ingest.

Like many bastards, he has lived far too long, and has been an explorer and adventurer, avid hunter, two-time winner of the Idi-tarod and scaler of mountains, travel scribe, and even a celebrity of sorts. When he is not the host of his cable show, *Blue Boy*—a popular series of interviews with visibly drugged rock stars, writers, and fellow expeditionists (the green-room candy bowls contain a mix of M&Ms, gummy bears with Molly centers, and peyote-dusted licorice), where he is never not entirely charming as his guests say what they never would otherwise—when he is not this, and when he is not lancing the world with his icepicks and crampons, he is something else. He is, in his big misunderstood heart, an artist.

He paints, though he rarely employs blue. Most of his works are muddied and reddish, and his new wife can discern, leaning into one of them on a cold night because he has demanded her opinion, that the paint is blood. It is possible that a small amount is hers, but she knows that the vials—he sometimes calls them "viles"—lined up on his studio shelves are filled with the blood of her predecessors. She understands, too, his earlier, mystifying comment, "Liquid Wife." She understands that to save her own life, she has to smile at him, as he stands with a dripping brush near a large in-progress canvas hooked to the wall, and give him encouragement.

"They are . . . astonishing," she says finally, locating the English word and turning back to look at him. He exhales, visibly relieved before recovering himself.

"Excellent," he says, playing with the brass buttons on his overalls. "Excellent."

———

The question she keeps coming back to is, How did she get here? She remembers—though it could as easily be a dream—a sour liquid he poured down her throat, and being pushed down a flight of stairs. Her pants ripped by a blade, a grappling for territory; attempted rape. It's possible her earlier life was excised when she banged her head as she fell. Images come to her: a woman's face, perhaps her mother's; a great river; a slithery black car that could be the one into which she was transferred during her abduction. Her languages, a Mandarin dialect and English, are intact, but not her name. In another of the images, she pushes a bowl of duck eggs, pickled and brown, toward an indistinct man. Her father, perhaps, or an uncle. Attempts to clutch the memories scatter them beyond reach. Gone are her treks to Tibet, that she had wanted at one time to be a Buddhist nun, that she had put gesang flowers behind her ear or was bitten by a snake that left two perfect punctures in her forearm or that one of her feet hosted a wart. When she sees the wart now, it seems only a meaningless feature. She does know that the sinister cloud in which she seems to be residing doesn't belong to her. She wonders who she is, having been born a second time into this particular prison.

When he addresses her at all, Blue usually calls her the Seventh. As for the rituals, he has left their marriage unconsummated and given her a bedroom separated from his by two rooms, one for sitting, one for dressing. His attempts so far at sexual congress have ended in recriminations from the book of the flaccid insane. She has puncture marks on her skin similar to the snakebite she doesn't remember; a burl of cigar ash sits in her foot like an enormous wart. Her skin is now a thing she notices, a permeable membrane alive with anticipations and hate.

Such is the map of her mind and her skin then; terra incognita on one side and, on the other, what she has come to think of as her situation.

———————

If the beard is examined with unfortunate intimacy, which is to say if one is surrounded and even smothered by it during an attack, one can see the range of hue, and somehow—even in the midst of receiving a belt buckle across the back or claws on the upper flesh of arms—detect the evocations of sky, the sea, certain birds, the largest whale in existence. The unexpected containment of things that shouldn't be contained. Or so she thinks, being one of his contained.

He paints and he paints and he paints but the images are never what he sees in his mind. What lands on his canvas is the attempt to relieve himself of his pain, which has something to do with being ignored when young. He puts Leonard Cohen on his playlist, approaches the vials and selects the deepest red he can find. What intrigues him is the similarity of red to red, the distinctions being nearly invisible to the untrained eye. He is able to tell the difference only through great familiarity, which proves his premise that the wives suffered, essentially, from a sameness induced by their destiny, their femaleness.

His hate, however, is inclusive, and in selecting his wives he has chosen from various countries and ethnicities. The wives have origins in Nigeria, Tanzania, Iran, Iceland, Thailand, India, and, lastly, China's Sichuan province, from which the Seventh was taken as she shopped in a busy market. The action of seizing her—three men, motorized scooters, and a bag over her head, all of it locally sourced and heavily funded—was simply absorbed by the crowds and caused only a momentary shriek and burst of down from a stack of caged birds. This is how easily a woman can disappear. She can be like the smoke rising from the woks and grills of the street food vendors. She can be plucked like a feather, even with a bag over her head and kicking. What people see in their periphery they assume is a bit of litter, a phantom or blown scarf or wing shadow; the muffled scream that they hear in their minds is something they consider to be their own damn business.

He selects the distillation of the Third and mixes it with a clear latex to stabilize it. He is keen to render a semblance of the once-living being and with a few flicks of his wrist bring her to life. Recognition for his talent, however, has been slow to be realized. His social-media follows and favorites are in the thousands and millions, and his videos, in which the wives are sometimes glimpsed (it is a game, catching the smudginess of them, an amorphous bit of leg, what might be a nipple), made viral (and, don't forget, even though there are the feminists who call him a raging misogynist and Inverted Smurf, there are the many fans who post pictures of their cats with blue beards), which pleases him. What he considers to be real success, however, the kind bolstered by respect, eludes him.

He drags his loaded brush across the surface primed with his special mix of grated plaster of Paris and rabbit glue (the rabbits, of course, he himself dispatched) and stands back to watch the reaction of his paint to the cold air and dust of his studio. He strokes his brush, hard, across the first mark, fixing his idea to the canvas, fixing her there. He will work for the next three hours before taking a long pull of his bourbon and relieving his desire in the bathroom.

———————

The house sits well north of Toronto where it can sprawl, bitten by black flies and raccoons, unimpeded. At night, the windows are black caves, full of hollow images, and have given each of the wives, when they were living, the sensation of being forever watched, ceaselessly scrutinized. Which, of course, they all were, though it is the Seventh who has had the bad luck to live in a time of general and highly advanced surveillance, such that the miniscule cameras, pinpricks of ogling so loved by the master, are in rich supply. They peer from twenty-eight positions throughout the mansion, the images transmitted to screens in a tiny room with one fat armchair, several bottles of Cristal in a refrigerator, and a box of tissues, the top layer of which one of the maids has fashioned into a blossom.

The cameras are useful for allowing him to keep up his living situation while he is off filming or chasing down toothy creatures. It is a life he loves, this pursuit of exotic spaces and living things, the dragging home of chattel. His boars, tigers, and lions are stuffed and posed in the living rooms; an Arctic wolf takes an endless dump outside one of the guest bathrooms and in place of the shit is a reposing Arctic hare. In the great hall, there are replicas of ships in glass and stuffed birds from Borneo. He has left dog sleds, canoes, bicycles, and horse saddles like litter, expedition tents hang to dry from kitchen chandeliers, and if someone pulls open a drawer, they will find binoculars and sextants and maps. They will find hair clippings and teeth and whole fingernails.

The Seventh files his nails, the very ones that hold wedged beneath them bits of her own skin; she is grinding her cells into a fine powder.

"What goes on in that head of yours, hmm?" he asks. She is unsure whether or not to answer him, as it is impossible to know which decision of hers will result in what he calls "provoking." The sum of his accusations is that she, by her very nature and presence, with each breath that comes in and out of her mouth, is the provocateur.

She settles on, "Sometimes my English fails me."

"The room is yours, of course, as they all are, and yet you haven't seemed enticed by it. So strange, your reticence, as if the curiosity isn't eating you alive."

He mentions the room often, almost daily, and she wishes he would stop. His fingers, his hands, his head, all of him seems gigantic to her and she hasn't gotten used to it in the weeks she's been here. His gaze, too, is outsized and peppery. "Is that a Chinese thing, do you think? The inscrutable Chinese, isn't that what they say?"

She pauses as if to configure her words. "I don't know." She thinks avengements, treacheries, annihilations. She thinks nail file straight into his enormous watery eyeball and into his brain.

"I think it's a place that would be of great interest to you. You've gone into every other room here—I've watched you. I have the footage." He reaches out to her face and just when she is expecting a slap or a pinch, he tucks a strand of her hair behind her left ear. "I will grant you this, however: that room does have a certain—how would you say—essence, and you've detected it."

She continues to file. He could drag her to the room, of course, but complicity is gold, so he decides on another route.

"Do you remember where you're from? Any of it? Well, best you don't. Chengdu is getting so polluted. You should thank me, bringing you here where the air is less . . . flocculent. Less beastly. Do you know an interesting quirk of your homeland? There are various curiosities I could enumerate, but at the top of the list is that, in spite of all the snake balls, bear penises, yak intestines, and frog skins your brethren eat, there is one creature in its own milieu. Try getting a permit to hunt a giant panda. Try getting one of those. They're protected! Can you believe that?" He snorts, which turns into a fit of coughs. He chases a pill with his whiskey but it's only a zinc tablet; the drugs he dispenses to those around him are only for those around him.

"One of my Chinese contacts said to me that the women of Sichuan are spicy, like the food. A handful, as it were. But that doesn't seem to be the case with you, does it? You're not much of a fighter." She focuses on the lateral swipes of the file, the hairs that curl out from the white French cuffs. She tries to ignore the hiss of his voice, the tiny drops of saliva that spray from his mouth and seem to spark when they hit her skin.

"You don't understand what I'm saying, do you? I could say anything, really. I could say, 'You nimble lightnings, dart your blinding flames / Into her scornful eyes! Infect her beauty, / You fen-sucked fogs drawn by the powerful sun, / To fall and blister!' I could say, 'Beware the Jubjub bird, and shun the frumious Band-ersnatch!' I could say anything at all, butterfly. But you just don't understand me."

She watches the file, which is the metal sort with a dull point at one end. Too dull perhaps, though it would depend on the area being penetrated. It is the kind of object whose simplicity in the right hands could render it lethal, depending on the angle of entry, depending on the vulnerability of the region being penetrated, depending on the fury behind the strike. Depending on any number of things.

The wives float in six cylindrical tanks. He singlehandedly doused the bodies first in formalin, then in streams of water, then in alcohol solutions of increasing strength until the final liquid of 80 percent. Let Damien Hirst try that, he has thought more than once. Another tank, empty, stands beside them in their neat row. Inside their fluid, the wives face various directions but hold the same vaguely fetal posture, legs slightly bent, their arms in front as if suspended while stopping an oncoming force, except that the hands are relaxed, turned inward, the fingers gently curled. Their heads are shaved and their skin, which has bleached over time, bears some resemblance to the squid and baby pigs—his practice pieces—that float in enormous jars nearby. He sees that Death has made them remarkably similar; their bodies in their respective tanks are uncannily alike, even though they have been arranged there, their decomposition suspended, one by one over many years. They have become the iterations of a single embryo: sisters. He appreciates this thought, the boost it gives him that, though they never met in life, they have the company in some sense of one another.

The bottoms and tops of the tanks are equipped with lights that are controlled from a small panel by the door, and recessed lighting stretches around the room's perimeter. He visits the room with less frequency now that he has the living one, the Seventh, to contend with. The empty tank collects dust while he works out what to do, while he tries to muster the urge to fill it and finds he is no longer quite so consistent, so avaricious. Perhaps, he thinks, he is simply getting old.

The Seventh stands outside the room with her hand on the door-knob, knowing what the room contains only because she has great sensitivity, even a touch of clairvoyance. She has dreamed, repeatedly, of the moon jellyfish at the aquarium in her other life, the one before she was taken. She would stand for hours looking at the undulating white ghosts and when they come to her now in her dreams she feels that the image connects in some way to the room's contents. All she has to do is open the door and step through.

She just stands there, however, debating with herself the consequence of being his viewer and their witness, until the sounds of the hounds being let out for their run startle her. She slips away down the corridors, heads for her upstairs room.

"You have to eat," he says, standing beside her as she sits at the dining table. The plates of what the kitchen staff reported she has waved away are lined up in a row. Shaved Brussels sprouts with blue cheese, foie gras on grilled brioche, fists of marinated pork loin hidden by nasturtiums, leeks stuffed with truffled potatoes, roasted plums with beeswax ice cream. "I could easily drum up some dog, if you like. Isn't that what your people eat?"

He immediately regrets saying this. The truth is that force-feeding her two days ago has rattled him; the straitjacket and strapping her down—which frankly should have aroused him—the rubber tubing and bags of Feast-Flo, the contortion of her jaw. Something has been changing in him and he can't bring himself to do it again. And yet, she is so slight, her skin seeming almost translucent. She is disappearing. There is a balance to be kept between breaking her and making her live. Perhaps she would be the one, eventually, to accept his nature, the things he feels compelled to do, actually love him. "Maybe it's noodles you want?"

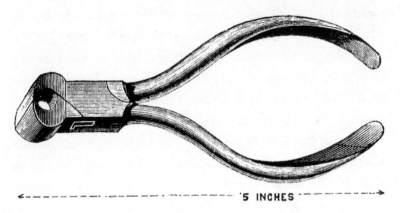

'5 INCHES'

FIG. 17.—CUTTING NIPPERS.

She stares at him. He notes that she never cries anymore, or shakes. He remembers placating his Icelandic wife with a little fermented shark and some puffin. "All this time I've been feeding you the wrong things. Let me talk to Cook. Something a little sweet and sour, yes? No? You're looking at me like I'm an imbecile—you think maybe I haven't—"

She can locate nothing to explain her current predicament, no goodness or badness, no philosophy of causation. She cannot locate the long evenings of doing her schoolwork while caring for her grandmother, or that she, age eight, had tried and failed to smother her infant cousin, because he was squalling and male and would thereafter receive every privilege. She panicked at his bluish lips, but she no longer remembers. She cannot remember the way she learned to use a cleaver to slice the softest bean curd into a cloud of threads, how the practice of slicing was a practice of the hand and the mind and the breathing; one slip and the threads would be ruined. Nor does she remember the American man she befriended during her freshman year at university, who said that a knife chopping said *fuck, fuck,* and she learned the word. She cannot locate the day she used the cleaver to slice into her thigh, how she breathed out the red line. She cannot locate what is fair or good or sinister or capricious because she cannot locate which of these she is.

Her body at times feels absurdly light, as if it isn't hers. She relinquishes it with each assault, so it is nothing Blue can take. The skin is something she longs to discard, and reclaiming it, then, is an act of defiance. She does not remember the Tibetan monk telling her that torture will make you sorry for your life, it will make you sorry you were born, he said.

She does not remember witnessing, a year later, the monk self-immolate on a busy road. He stopped his devotions on a particularly hazy day to find a space on the pavement. Then: a shower of gasoline from his plastic canister, the sound of his match. A gathering crowd held up their phones to record the body of the monk. They watched the way the body eventually tipped while holding the lotus position, a frozen shadow inside the agitated flame. He was not there, he was not there at all. But she does not remember.

———————

What she sees out her bedroom window is evidence of a terrible continuity; the sky is unchanging, undisturbed, and it never seems to rain. The windows don't open and she has tried every single one of them. (He enjoys this the most, seeing the impact of his terrorizing; not only the impact, but the inner workings, the *mechanics*, the way that one act on his part will produce in his victims' heads myriad fear-soaked computations. It is a system that runs itself.)

She knows this, the game of echoes, but it doesn't mitigate the anxiety that sips away at her oxygen. She wonders if the doors were suddenly opened, if she—or any of the others—would flee or if, in the manner of a trained elephant held by a small loop of rope, she would think her next life, the one of liberation, to be impossible.

The odd memories that do come to her are senseless postcards from someone she no longer knows. Her consciousness has awakened to find the body bruised, scabbed, her blood reactive to the mere sound of Blue's footsteps, his scrubby breathing. The hot snap of a belt in the frigid air.

She doesn't remember the Buddhist nun who taught her during a retreat to meditate, but the lesson of stilling the mind, of being inside the body, even if the body is slapped or burned, is suddenly there as she closes her eyes in her bedroom. The body that he ravages seems to be the very creature she has to fully inhabit if she wants her freedom. Which, despite how inadequate to the task she feels, she does.

———————

He has told her to visit the seamstress, Tuk, while he is at work because her clothes are loose—and he himself has shredded some of them—and so she walks through the corridors, through the invisible gaze of cameras nine through thirteen. She taps at the door, and the seamstress—blind, stocky, smiling—appears. Tuk looks at her directly and seems to see her, even though the Seventh knows better. The sewing room, which is also where Tuk sleeps, is kept dark and the shades drawn because she doesn't need the light, and therefore it is one of the only rooms Blue doesn't monitor or visit.

"Do you want the lights?" Tuk asks, as always, but the Seventh replies, "No," as always. She craves the dark and that quick, hot touch as she is measured and fitted. She raises her arms when Tuk prompts her to, and this is a bit like floating, since it is dark, and there are hands at her ribs, gently. Tuk unfastens buttons and zippers; the Seventh feels the air on her breasts, the fingers sliding over her, reading her. Tuk's breathing is audible as she finds the marks and variations.

"This is a terrible inventory," she says, "finding what he's done to you now." The Seventh has welts on her back, a swelling on her right hip, and since she is losing weight, her pubic bone—hairless because Blue has shaved her—protrudes under the skin and it is the spot where Tuk eventually brushes her mouth.

The rumor about Tuk is that Blue stole her from her cradle twenty years earlier as an act of revenge while he was on an expedition in a northern latitude. A generous Inuit family hosted him and one evening cut up a seal to share with him on their kitchen floor; they offered him, as their honored guest, everything from the whiskers to the liver to the tender brain, pieces of which swam in a metal pan with some blood and fat. The elderly matriarch of the family offered the pan to him and he ate from it with his fingers, as he knew to do, before giving his thanks and, when it was time to flee and the family members were otherwise occupied, he tucked the baby, small and fat and glossy-eyed, into the fur lining of his coat. Fleeing, of course, meant sledges and snowmobiles and pontoon planes and several days of travel. When he finally reached home with her he dubbed her Tuk, a name he chose simply for the comfort of its sound. Because he is repulsed by her blindness—the result of a childhood fever—he has been reluctant to be near her, unless a fitting is required, much less beat or molest her, though she is enslaved all the same.

———————

The Seventh holds Tuk between her thighs. She asks, because the question has been forming around them, "Do you think of killing him?" She thinks at first that her question is rhetorical, but as she hears herself say the words, she decides she wants to hear the answer. She touches Tuk's face, but feels her fingers being pushed away, the space around her becoming colder.

"No," says Tuk. "Never."

———————

Tuk can remember, a little, what seeing was like before she was blinded. She remembers the fever at five years of age that made the world around her seem dry and brittle, as if her bed, the nurse tending her, and the dark figure in the doorway could be crumbled, and how, when she woke up blind one morning, she was unsurprised. The only relief was not having to see that beard again or the man attached to it. He had made some of her beloveds disappear, she knew, and perhaps he had even caused the whole world to be swallowed by shadow.

It was Blue's Chief Assistant who placed a box of needles and thread into her small hands and whispered into her ear that she would transcend her loss of sight, she would be gifted. He hoped so at any rate, because he had plans for her. One day she hemmed Blue's pants and Blue was surprised at the invisible stitches, and even more intrigued after he mockingly commanded her to produce a shirt for him, which two days later she presented. Years went by and she found herself kneeling at the feet of the Sixth on the day of the wedding, stitching last-minute seed pearls into the lace. She realized that the movement of the dress was being caused by the Sixth's trembles. Another year passed and suddenly the Sixth was gone, and no one said a thing about her, not even to explain to Tuk why she wasn't coming for her wardrobe fittings. Tuk hid in her room for as long as she could before Blue bellowed that a new dress had to be made, and so her work began again.

It was after the arrival of the Seventh that the Chief Assistant, now on the verge of being an elderly man and aware that time was closing, paid Tuk another visit, this time to bestow a pair of scissors. "You are grown now, and the time has come," the Chief said. He hung the scissors so that they hid openly on the sewing room wall, next to the other scissors and tape measures and spools. Tuk repeatedly felt around the wall for them, memorizing their location. They seemed to her perfectly ordinary.

———

Blue watches the Seventh from ledges and window casings and bookshelves, from ceiling lights and paintings and taxidermy. But his favorite camera, which gives him a view of her toilet and tub, is burrowed in the eye socket of a ceramic cupid residing on her bathroom vanity. Sometimes he has the stills turned into drink coasters or playing cards and distributes them to his poker friends, or sometimes he sells the footage to the highest bidder at secret auctions. Sometimes he sees that she hides behind pieces of furniture, which is oddly charming (does she suppose that he can't see her?), or moves the location of one of his little statues of naked women, the ones that sit between stacks of books or prop doors open or hold down reams of paper.

Sometimes the audio will pick up what seems to be humming. It is the sound she makes as she moves into the smallest, darkest space in her mind, shuts herself inside. The self, as large as it is, as expansive and wandering, as tentacled, can be squeezed down to a particle of grit. This is the best, most secret ability she has.

———

It will happen any day now, her rescue. The fire trucks, loaded with men and hoses, will come, the police with their guns drawn, the SWAT teams of free women swinging on cables, feet thrust out to obliterate the triple-paned glass of the enormous windows. There will be sirens peeling a strip out of the low-hanging sky as the sound rips through. There will be megaphones and spotlights sweeping the ground, people in uniforms shrieking orders, and ambulances full of syringes, oxygen tanks, and defibrillators, and a gurney onto which she will be forced—and which she will resist only because she has had no reason to trust anyone in this place. There will be more cameras, and their crews and reporters, and yellow caution ribbons containing the whole business and everyone in it. Someone will say her name as the ambulance doors swing wide and a shoulder-mount camcorder sniffs at her pores. They will say her real name and not the one he gave her—they will say Wen or Shu or Mei Lin and she will say Yes, that is my name. I am she, and all the way to the hospital there will be a cacophony of sirens, orders, rain (at last the rain) slapping the windshield, and above everything a terrifying syncopation that she realizes suddenly is her heart.

But no. Just no. That isn't the way it happens.

He isn't actually going to kill her, not right this minute. However, as his hand grips her throat and her feet almost lift off the floor, he is able, he thinks, to nearly see into her mind. Except the secret self, so small and quick, is beyond his reach. He is unaware of what exactly it is he is trying to pry loose from her. He only knows that something, whatever it is, flies about inside her with such unbounded freedom that the idea of it sours his stomach. His fingers, huge around her little neck and clawing into what flesh she has, squeeze along the jugular. It is like holding a kitten or one of his piglets. Her vulnerability sends a rush of adrenaline through him, which makes him hard, and he contemplates how to make her duly afraid. Because he understands something now, holding her there by the neck and seeing her beginning to struggle to breathe, her small fingers lightly beginning to clutch at his as if she could loosen his grip. He can see, unexpectedly, that she is not nearly as frightened as he would like her to be.

Practice, practice, practice.

Many years ago, after one of his expeditions had run into trouble, his rescuers pulled up in a cargo ship to find him lounging on an ice floe, sucking on the tail of a seal. He burst out laughing and didn't stop as they carried him up the ship's gangway. Some said his cruelty was born on that expedition, but others knew well enough that he was disturbed long before the journey north and before he ever married. He had drowned puppies as a child and was thought not to mind terribly when his sled dogs had to be shot in the head, one by one, and eaten. Had the other expedition members survived, however, they could have attested to the fact that he'd bellowed and sobbed when the lead dog, Surly, was mutinously taken out, and screamed when Bear was next, and threatened to shoot them or himself in the head if they took Sir Guff, which they did. He didn't fire any shots, however; he watched them starve and outlived them all instead.

Barely on the ship, he recounted for the captain how a group of Inuit had found him only two days before but had left him to die (they had thought naturally enough that the ridiculous beard of blue meant *something*, and so they disappeared over the ice and snow). He howled with laughter because, he said, one day he would return and seek revenge. "Because I'm a connoisseur of abduction," he shrieked. "A fucking connoisseur!"

He has tried meditating but it doesn't stop the rage. He has tried antidepressants and psychoanalysis and hobbies (threw his hockey skates out a window, bludgeoned his patch of butter lettuce, stabbed a housekeeper's regrettable thigh with his knitting needles). Still, it comes, and he is overtaken with the urges, with how much sense they make—with how much sense *he* makes—until he has found himself dragging the body of another of his wives through the corridors, over stones shipped from Madagascar and Afghanistan, down the set of stairs carved into the limestone foundation by local artisans, into the tiled room where he would begin to prepare the body. Wives one through six. His favorite was the Second, imported from a seaside Icelandic village and not the smartest of the bunch (which didn't surprise him as she was so terribly blonde) but she laughed easily, was more than competent in bed, and put up a good fight in the end. The First was special because she was, well, the first, and bad-tempered and spoke only in an Indian dialect in which he was barely proficient; their conversations were brief and laced with hand gestures. The Third, by contrast, had been a linguistics professor who spoke four languages and who begged for books to read at night; her death had been the most satisfying. The Fourth died, he swore, more from the consequence of a terrible flu rather than his own hands, but she would have said otherwise. The Fifth fell apart in his grasp as easily as breaking a biscuit and it still enraged him. The Sixth wife: she was from Thailand, but her meditations didn't help her in the end; she was obligated to him, he was quick to observe, because he had hustled her on to her next life.

Thereafter he did consider the benefits of working on mental balance and even invited a Franciscan brother to the house for instruction. The brother, who was young and unopposed to the vagaries of the internet and social media (and, in fact, found the online world to be as viable or not as any other), took one look at @beardofblue's account and never showed up. #divineintervention.

The thing is, what really ignites his rage is the incompetency all around him; a sea of staff and wives, none of whom have seemed remotely capable of stopping him, who are, in fact, complicit because of their weaknesses, their victimhood, their passive-aggressive hatred. He knows they hate him, that behind all the bowing and scraping and falling silent when he enters a room is a fetid, percolating hate, and yet it isn't enough to induce their rebellion, at least not one more interesting than their ineffectual attempts to ruin his day, like oversalting his food or taking too long to unplug his toilet. There is only one of him and yet they still can't do it, turn that frisson of excitement (because surely they must have it, too, somewhere within them, the thrill experienced while wishing to stomp his face in) into a unifying plot to poison him (how hard could it be?), shoot him in the back, or smash his skull with a lead statue, baseball bat, tire iron. Honestly—and he says the word out loud before he drains the whiskey from his highball—*honestly*, they deserve to do his bidding if they cannot drag their own horror, their own true weakness, into the light.

Speaking of weakness, every monster has an Achilles' heel (*Mother-fuckers' Bestiary and Compendium*, look it up). His is that he suffers from a kind of sleep paralysis. One night, about 1:15 a.m., he opens his eyes and gasps. It is Tuk's round face that he sees, hovering over him. She tells him to stay very still as she straddles him.

"You can't touch me," she says, and he believes her. The room is suddenly frigid and her breath silver in the moonlight. He has always been a little afraid of her, not so much because of her curious abilities but that blind, unsettling face.

She finds his nightshirt unbuttoned as she lets her fingertips touch down like a concert pianist. The hairs of his chest are surprisingly soft. He smells like a doused bonfire and even vaguely skunkish. She feels for his griffin hands, which lie on either side of his body, completely limp. She reaches for the scissors that are tucked into her belt and pictures them glinting when she holds them up.

"I'm only doing an experiment," she whispers, pulling on a section of his beard. In her mind's eye, she has the image of the hairs, embellished with the Seventh's description of them. She feels him aroused between her legs, even through the heavy quilts, the ones she has helped to stitch, the ones that hold patches of the wives' gowns.

"You have to be still! It is essential." She thinks that perhaps he can't speak—she tries to remember exactly what the Chief Assistant told her but this detail escapes her.

"Haven't I been like a father to you, Tuk? Wouldn't you like to put the scissors down?"

She steadies herself, her thighs gripping him. She wonders if her hatred for him means she can't take advantage of her position, for a moment or two. She could ride him, or snip off his prick, or both! She could plunge the scissor blades straight down into his chest. She understands, however, the limitations with which this opportunity has been endowed and the object, so said the Chief Assistant, is to collect that piece of his beard. It is the only way, though she does not know why this would be so, why it has to be so bloodless. His breastplate begs to be shattered, his heart ripped out, his eyes plucked from his head. How can it possibly be that the way to end everything is with a gesture, the sort she makes every day, made almost absurd by its mundanity? But the Chief Assistant, the one closest to Blue and most initiated in the logic of this place, said so. He said that a brief power outage would disable the cameras so she could move through the hallways unrecorded, and he warned her, too, that the fine hairs have the toughness of steel cables, but she is ready, having already sharpened the scissors assiduously. She growls, "You don't know how lucky you are."

"Fuck you," Blue says, as she grabs the hairs tighter—all those wondrous filaments of sky and ocean—they even smell of the sea—they're smelly like seals! She holds them in her calloused fingers, which shake a little. The scissors feel suddenly large and awkward, but swish through the hairs as easily as snipping silk thread.

Just as the Chief Assistant had told her would happen, the act of cutting solves the conundrum of her escape—he is instantly asleep, back in his lurid dreams. She smooths his beard to hide the missing piece and leans into his ear, "You will think me a dream," and she knows it to be true.

The nature of the universe, whose very components she clutches in her fist, is altering, and every mysterious thing distills to one sensation: her bare feet hitting the stones of the dark hall as she flees.

The Chief Assistant, after learning of Tuk's success and who has been waiting for the collapse of this nightmarish existence for decades, expects that the blue bastard will groom his beard in the sanctity of his private commode, find that a transgression has occurred, and drop to the floor, *fini*. The Chief Assistant is certain that that is what will happen, yes, quite certain, based on his calculations and research and consultations, and yet Blue keeps appearing at breakfast, lunch, and dinner, and he appears to be the same sonofabitch as ever.

Even if the Chief Assistant has lost confidence, Tuk has not. She comes in and out of Blue's bedroom, feeling her way with one hand while carrying in the other arm his pants and jackets, ones she has just finished tailoring but finds she has to redo because he seems to have lost weight. Or, as she puts it, "shrunk."

He watches her steadily, not with his usual omnivorous glower but as though waiting to see her next move. She smiles at him, seeming to look directly into his eyes, and makes little jokes as she runs a Braille tape measure down the inside of his legs or bites off thread between her teeth. She merrily stacks his dress shirts in her arms and takes them away, giving him one last grin at the door and the Seventh an absurd wink. They both watch her saunter down the hall and Blue notes that she doesn't feel her way. "She is whistling," he says.

The first signs appear as subtle disturbances in his concentration. He looks up from his ratings reports or his maps or his issue of *ARTnews* as if he'd heard something in the distance or winces while eating like he's bitten his cheek. Even his rages take on a different character and his inflection changes mid-roar. He gathers his fingers around the Seventh's throat, but hasn't the will to even complete his sentence. He grows more incoherent and undecided, and even though the changes are vague, over the course of two weeks confusion settles into his face, lending his rages a tenor of meekness, something even like innocence.

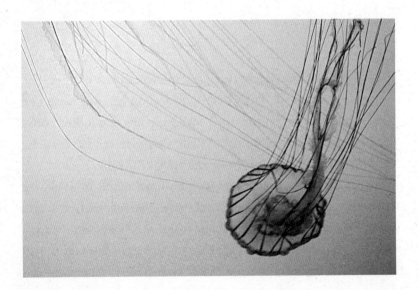

11

Walking among the wives, she notices, is not entirely different from walking through a museum. Except that competing with the role of observer is a dark spot forming just below her sternum, a small encumbrance that begins to rumble quietly, the opening seed of a howl. The Seventh tries to steady herself as she moves among the tanks and their soft electrical buzzing.

One of the wives is tall compared to the others, another's mouth is slightly parted revealing a missing tooth on the bottom row, another's fingernails are still attached and painted. She wonders about their true names as she looks at the placards, which have been neatly lettered: *First*, *Second*, *Third*, *Fourth*, *Fifth*, and *Sixth*. The empty tank has an empty placard and the blankness seems like a waiting thing, though, she thinks, perhaps not necessarily for her. She is disgusted with herself when she entertains, briefly, a modicum of hope.

Blue is sipping cognac and catching up on several episodes of his private reality show, *The Seventh Hour*. The footage from that particular room, the one with the tanks, is always bothered by an inexplicable static, making her halting steps grainy. It elates him, though, to have the first viewer of his most complex work, to see how it staggers her and how she composes herself. She continues around the tanks, peering up into the wives' almost impassive faces (he attempted to give each of them an expression somewhere between melancholia and beginning to understand a good joke, an aspect vague enough to provoke among viewers an argument over what, exactly, they are conveying in their faces), and placing her fingers over her lips. She stops and stares, observing the empty, unlit tank. He watches her startle and look toward the door as if she expects someone to step through, and then return to walking around the tanks. He watches as she leaves the frame of the video, wills her to come back into view; silently pleads for her return. He hasn't expected the drop of sadness, perhaps something even like remorse, that accumulates on the tip of his conscience, or the strange sort of longing he feels, which is truly a first.

———————

And it doesn't last long. He storms through the corridors, kicking debris, shoving open doors, slamming them. She has forced his hand—he has to complete his work. Even as he had invited her to look, even as he kept the door unlocked so that she could fulfill her destiny as viewer. Even so.

He goes in search of his camera, which he much prefers to his phone for documentary purposes (and think of the viral possibilities!), but when he reaches his studio he discovers it isn't there. He circles around, searching his brain for when he last held the camera. He staggers out the double studio doors, frightening one of the hounds that is lapping water from a large bowl. He shoves the hound, dashes the bowl against the wall, all the while beginning to feel that coming unhinged will impede both of his tasks—he knows this from experience—for the neatest killing requires that his rage be honed, and photographing her body requires another kind of clarity. Even with vibration reduction in his lenses, he needs a steady hand. It is all an art.

*   *   *

The problem is the malaise that has been consuming him. He feels unusual, but can't place the sensation. His vision dims momentarily and he seems as blind as Tuk. His heart beats much too fast, then barely seems to pump, and the corridor, the hound, the stones, his rage merge in an enervating, sickening swirl and he finds he can no longer run. When he opens the door to his library, he sees, instead, his wife.

"I can't find it!" He pivots in various directions, his claws at his chest.

The Seventh takes a step back. "What are you looking for?"

"The—you know!" His gaze darts back and forth as he searches for the missing word for the missing item. "The—the whatsit—the—motherfucker!"

She smiles as the memory of reading Thich Nhat Hanh comes back to her. "Perhaps it is yourself you seek." She startles herself by laughing out loud.

"Are you losing your mind?" He pats his torso while still searching around. "If I could just find—"

He takes a step toward her but his eyes are wide. She stays still. It occurs to her that possibly she *is* losing her mind. He has infected her body, and now her brain. Madness might be the conversion of fear, or the loss of it, or perhaps this is what enlightenment is; or madness and enlightenment are one and the same. She registers geese out past the gardens and a delivery truck pulling away. He staggers and she steps clear. It is like a dance. He drops to one knee. She hears the toenails of the hounds scrape the floor above as they run, she hears the blood of every person in the house, but she can barely hear him. He mouths something, presumably, "Help me." He extends his arms but can't reach her.

She bends to hover out of reach of the face that has so oppressed her. "I don't understand what you're saying," she says. "No, I don't understand you."

A flicker on his sweating face. She watches him, fascinated by how the rage fights for time with his helplessness.

"You seem to be—you taught me this word, you know— laconic. It's beautiful, isn't it? What is the English phrase? *Words escape you.* Very poetic, yes? The idea of escape, in a place like this."

His gaze is fixed on her and then it isn't. The other knee touches down and he tips, gently at first, until his face smacks the floor. A ripple through him, as if giant hands are holding his head and whipping out his body. The hounds above go wild as the butler yells for them to settle down. Blue exhales and is suddenly still and heavy on the ground.

Any moment she expects the colossus to roar up, but nothing happens. Or rather, many things happen inside him unseen. She swears that she hears the silence following the last tick of his heart. The hounds are suddenly quiet, and she waits, to make sure he is dead, a full fifteen minutes—she watches the clock that serves as the head on a naked porcelain woman—before slipping out of the room.

She runs to find Tuk to tell her that he is dead, but when she stands in the door of Tuk's little room and feels an absence, she flicks on the light. She sees the organized debris of a carefully arranged exit. The sewing machines are there, the boxes of needles and thread,

and the measuring tapes are still draped on their pegs. The bed has been carefully made and the clothing ironed and stacked. On the wall close to the door is the raised outline of a pair of scissors and within the outline, nothing.

The Seventh has Tuk's tape measure in her pocket as she sits on a chair in the dining room. Someone has placed a coarse blanket around her shoulders, and a pair of journalists stands nearby. One of them munches an apple while the other reads to him the names from a list of missing women and they try to guess which ones might be the wives. She has yet to hear a name that is familiar to her, that she knows belongs to her. A nurse gently feels for her wrist to take her pulse; the Seventh however, will slip away before she lets them put her in the ambulance that waits outside. They can record her pulse, take her blood pressure, make notes of the scabs and scars, but they cannot have her. She will race over the grass that she has only seen from the windows and never felt, she will disappear into the forest that climbs rolling hills and contains, somewhere, a blind seamstress who waits for her.

An officer, she realizes, is trying to take her statement. The questions are repetitive, perfunctory. He asks when she first arrived here, he asks when she last saw Blue, he backtracks and asks who she is. She stares at him, waiting for him to blink his pale eyes. No one, it seems, can tell her her name. She grabs the shirt of the officer—"Whoa now!"—and pulls him closer. He calls her ma'am, puts his hand firmly, too firmly, over hers, and tells her to be patient. He's seen this before, however, and he feels badly. He turns to the nurse and says how understandable it is. They both nod: of course, of course. "Because really," he says to the nurse, whom he sees has a fetchingly crooked smile and it occurs to him just then that she would make a good mother, "because really, when you think about it, she could be anybody."

———————

After the six bodies are clumsily extracted from the tanks—a process more arduous and undignified than even the ones doing the extracting anticipated—six hearses arrive. They sit, freshly polished, on the paving stones and wait for the women, who are brought out on gurneys one by one by silent people and lifted in. The hearses slowly pull out, a broken line of shining black, and move down the long driveway and around the curve until they disappear. Police officers and reporters, even one of the hounds, gather on the front lawn and watch them go. Somewhere in the back gardens, beyond the rose bushes and sycamores and cypresses, the other hounds start to yowl, the sound expanding up over the eaves and roof tiles. The hound tips back its nose and considers whether to sing out in that collective mourning, for the master is gone, or to take the form of the ancestral creature whose spirit now floods his DNA. He breaks into a run. Wolf it is.

. . . *and she was still afraid of Jupiter, and was fearful of her being stolen, until she gave her to Argus, the son of Ariston, to be kept by him.*

—OVID, *METAMORPHOSES*

KITES

1.

The shot comes seemingly from nowhere, a quick needle through her abdomen, clean, and not the wreckage of the hollow-point round or a point-blank shot. Then the sound—in his mind it seems to arrive almost after the hit—and her body folding to the concrete against the pull of his arm. She had been leaning against him, her head thrown back, laughing at what he'd said. What had he said? So light, except when she falls. The movement of her body counterclockwise—unwind this action—his clutching at her, transferring her blood to his shirt, like the art his daughter makes by pressing paint between two sheets of paper, which she pulls gleefully, triumphantly apart.

2.

He gets up to run. He doesn't turn to register the dazzling confusion of her face, its stricken deportment, hung as she is on the hook of an almost painless surprise. He isn't certain that she says anything, makes any noise whatsoever, though it is possible that his first steps away from her have rendered him deaf. The first steps are dream steps, sticky and slow. Then better.

He wonders who to ask for help, but can't keep a thought. Too many stairs to count. Hard to assemble the forms of so many people. The streets at a distance are full of them. Even though he thinks of a crowd as uncaring (how many of his patients, after all, have met violence surrounded by people?), he imagines that if he screams and hollers, someone has to stop and help. And help.

Glancing down a side street, he sees a hundred red leaves flurry out from a tree in a single burst. Leaves like an arterial explosion.

3.

No one will help a cracker with a bloody imprint on his button-down. The city seems out of reach, slipping through. He runs hands over chest to make sure it's true that the one hit is not him. The city is a slot machine of actions and reactions, you never know what it will do. He bellows to a veritable chasm that she's been shot.

No, he doesn't do that. In the still center of the vortex he realizes that he need never say the words at all.

4.

He thinks of his patients in the emergency room: the man with the nail in his skull who asked if he could watch television, the teenage girl who handed him a urine sample and apologized that it was full of blood, the terminal boy who wanted to know why his dead grandmother was there at the end of the bed.

Couldn't he, after all, turn around—

5.

In the city are pockets of solitude, emptiness, and you can see in the cross streets the taxis gliding, a crowd beyond the buildings up ahead. He wants to reach them and make them hear him, understand his position. He would like to make a plea, but the noises drown him out. A city in sound, sirens and screams, buses' pneumatic hiss.

6.

Several feet away from her are someone's corduroy sofa, a recycling bin, stacks of cardboard neatly tied with twine. There is even a bow, double-knotted. And the shards of a broken bottle that have been ground down so much they sparkle.

As he stumbles along, he feels his heart clobbering his chest, how it wants to undo itself, escape his body. There is nothing wrong. He is among them now, the others.

7.

There are a few strangers who look at him and his guilty shirt, a few who divert their paths, and one trashcan that he nearly topples, but otherwise he moves among them like a shadow. They are going to work, or going home or to the dentist or to a tryst. He feels the rasp of drying blood against his skin. Her face in his mind as he half walks, half runs. An animal he doesn't want to see. Encapsulated in her rounded mouth and the curvature of the wound, the surprise of dying suddenly. A silent sustained *Oh!* Her expression, its particular distance, a familiar one to him. Once that metamorphosis has settled in—the death look—it ticks off the minutes at an inexorable pace until the end is irrevocably there. She is something else entirely.

He would take it back.

8.

Meeting her today. He had had doubts for months; it was petering out, he knew. And she had sensed it, which was why she laughed so easily at his joke. She may have been constructing her own apologia. Here is a phrase that people say: *out of nowhere.* Sometimes there isn't a genesis that can be named. Sometimes transformation just happens.

He should have ended it months ago. His wife had begun to hunt through his pockets, his top drawer, his phone. He would have ended it, if it weren't for—what?

Inside the erotic triangle, the pinpoint of annihilation, its addicting scrutiny.

9.

The act of leaving is a force that grows in power the farther away from her he gets. It propels him through the crowd in which he wants to wash himself clean. He cannot slow his heart, shore his brain, stop himself from leaving her. The rift, now nine city blocks in diameter, is wide open and sutureless.

epilogue

In exchange for the city drinking him down and letting him get away with his escape: his nightly search for sleep, trying to stab it down with a fist screwed into the pillow. The city commiserates, however; it understands the unsettled soul. It always forgives.

The start of evening will unfold this way for him, regardless of season; with the blood of the descending sun, and those indifferent hordes through the cross streets. He will always notice the detritus of leaving. The overstuffed trashcans, bundled cardboard, abandoned furniture. Kites of litter.

*The wandering bird, too, having long sought for land, where it may be
allowed to light, its wings failing, falls down into the sea.*

—OVID, *METAMORPHOSES*

SEA OF LOVE

The house is different after the storm, and by storm I mean hurricane.
Entire towns on the east coast were swallowed, digested, thrown
back up. The house is different, though it has changed less than
I have. The shallow basement contains sand, and the first floor
has a waterline that runs a shade dark two feet from the ceiling.
The water is long gone now, but it altered everything it touched,
even invisible things. It changed marriages. It did this by sheer
force, maybe, or by surprise. Creatures were left for a time in our
kitchen and living room, including a jellyfish, brown and purple
as a wet bruise, slumped on an armchair and urchins that clung
to the drapes. The water had come in as a king tide, and when
it receded, grey and magnetic, I was in it. Seduced. I watch my

husband and the woman he is with now as he putters around the house, and I hover about the walls while the dogs' ears twitch.

The buildup to the storm took several days. The weather forecaster was the edifying kind and described how the winds started in East Africa, sped up over the mountains, and crossed the Sahara before arriving at the Atlantic. "Imagine feeling the sea after the desert," she said. I watched her face on my computer screen and imagined that someone in the control room was telling her to hurry it along. The storm grew as it crossed the water and enraptured satellites watched its path. When it came close to the east coast, my husband suggested we go to the grocery store, but I said the lines would be long. He said they would only get longer. When we got there, we saw people enlivened with purpose, some of them crowding a tower of batteries and water bottles, avid as gulls. Nobody knew what the dervish would do, how big it would get and whether it would go or stay.

I wanted it to stay. The storm had grown a name and, even more thrilling, it opened its eye, wide. It resembled slightly the cyclone on Jupiter, which has egotistically raged for more than three hundred years. You got the sense that it saw what it wanted to do, how it wanted to gouge the coast with wind. People spoke of leaving their homes, and abandonment hung in the air. But when the hurricane got to shore it was only a category one with speeds of 85 mph. More than the wind, it was the water that did the damage. The current in some places was a terrible train and carried away docks, SUVs, and the wild horses of Sable Island. For days before it came, you could hear boards being hammered in place, people heaving sandbags. Futile, most of it. A game of whack-a-mole against a torrent that could flood any space it pleased. I remember that I stood on the front porch in my nightgown, with boots on my feet and water climbing the sides of them. My husband—I'm not sure where he was. I will call him Ahmed. No, Gerome. He was somewhere.

In the early days of our marriage, he said something unusual. It caught me off-guard because I considered him uninteresting, but had married him anyway; or maybe I married him because of it. I had sliced my wrist—this was only an accident I think—and we sat in an emergency room. A nurse wrapped my arm in bandages and then left to take care of other people. My blood appeared on the surface and spread. I wanted to feel something about it, apart from a twinge that I was different from the other patients, who were so engrossed in their calamities that they didn't hear when their names were called. A pair of teenage boys moaned in unison and an old woman shouted marvelous curses in French. Over by the vending machine, a couple—stoned maybe and wracked by laughter—tried to feed coins into it. The room was lit by stabbing fluorescents, alive with suffering. My husband ignored it all, except the bandages. He said, "White contains everything, including nothing." I wanted to write it down, but it was my writing hand that was bandaged. I thought that he would never say another thing like it, but I didn't have to worry. When we got home from the hospital, he was agitated and rooted through the kitchen drawers until he found a notebook and a pen. He held them up triumphantly, as if they would have made any difference at all.

Before the house near the ocean, we lived on a great lake so polluted that someone developed a roll of film in it. I don't know what objects or people were in the pictures, just that someone developed the roll. After that, we decided the ocean would be healthier and found a house that smelled of saline and had a view of the water from the second floor. One of the first things I did was race upstairs and peer from the bedroom windows with the avidity of a stalker. I swam every day through the summers until the water turned frigid and drove me out. The winters were hard and crystalline, and when the air was sufficiently cold, it made starbursts all over the car's windshield. People whose lust was even bigger than mine still went in the water and surfed through January and February. They wore black wetsuits and one day we could hear them hooting with cold when they came back in to shore. My husband said he envied them and bought a wetsuit the following week, but I never saw him in it, not even once.

Our marriage had what you might consider two lives. The first time we were together his mother gave us six months, and we made it six years just to spite her. The day that we divided everything up, our packing was so amicable that she wept in frustration. It was a Sunday afternoon, something like a dream, and the people in it resembled friends, relations. They helped us pass our boxes and furniture into a pair of vans, but nobody spoke except to say thank you. We were enveloped in a blandness so sleep-inducing that we forgot to get a divorce. The papers sat on my kitchen counter, marked by coffee rings and pomegranate splashes, and turned yellow at the edges. On a bright summer day, I rolled them into a tube and used them to smack a fly, before I smoothed them out again.

The house and the ocean, more than the marriage, stayed in my head. A year later, when my husband showed up at my work with an armful of too-white lilies and roses and said, "Come back," I said, "Where to?" He said the house was back on the market and it could be ours again. I thought about my love for the burnished floorboards, the elderly cupboards, the windows that were thicker at the bottom where the glass had slowly pooled over all the years of their existence. Moreover, I considered the ocean—glinting, predatory—and understood that my desire was narrow and absolute. I heard myself say, "Well, yes," and we went to a hotel to negotiate the terms. In the morning he tore my brioche into small pieces and I poured his coffee. I was disappointed to learn as we nibbled breakfast that his mother had already had a heart attack in the previous year and that they had fixed the valve. She was stronger than ever, he said. "Like a brick shithouse with a moat around it." He sipped at his coffee and seemed to be thinking, but I don't know what about.

The house was more or less the same when we moved back in. The cedar shingles have weathered like wolf fur and the trim is painted tooth white. A red door. Still, it has never seemed a voracious place. A neighbor told us a red door was pointless because it would be beaten by sun and salt, which it was. It has ended up the color of liver. Inside the house, there are canvas-covered sofas, and armchairs whose legs are too long, and there are bowls for the dogs—the names are missing, but say they are Sigmund and Freud. They patiently wait for the woman to drop the steak she is eviscerating. She doesn't look at the ocean much, even though it waits, as the dogs do, for another opportunity.

———

I considered the process of going home again, which they say is an unfeasible thing. You wonder what home is, and what it wants. Your own expectations have changed a little, enough to mean that you aren't the same and neither is the home. The floors are off-kilter, the drafts rush your skin like bees, and the foundation has an ebony gap that weeps. The look in your eye has gone metallic, and the house hardly knows you and the extra five pounds you carry when you stomp up and down the stairs. You find yourself envying the porch on the neighbor's house.

The woman—I will call her Estelle—looks very much like one of the neighbors who lived a few houses down. She seems to reside here now, lying without hesitation on chaises, on the bed. Her toothbrush sits in a cup in the upstairs bathroom. Her bathing suit is languid on the shower rod. She has three handbags in the front hallway closet and a battered copy of *The Odyssey*—mine, which had somehow survived the storm—in the recycle bin. (Homer has

Leódês say, "'Never have / I word / Injurious spoken, or injurious deed / Attempted 'gainst the women of thy house.'")

The dogs are close by, too. Large, with long eyelashes and black, almost purplish, snouts. They lie near the door, wanting to be taken out, while my husband massages the feet of Estelle. I can move around the room, I can become the whole house and only twice have the dogs stirred. One stood up and cocked his head, but I drew myself into the window panes and he settled. There is a cat, too, though it isn't mine. A calico with a fogged eye, like a bottle left outside, and cross ears.

My husband stirs his coffee, he speaks with Estelle, he arranges his paperwork, but he imagines that I'm with him. This is the problem—or the advantage—of love, even the insufficient kind, and also with death. I'm bigger than I ever was. I still long for a roiling, capricious power, however; the Grace of the Witch. I change with the best of them, draw myself to the front door and listen to the sounds of scurrying creatures, though I don't remember what they are. I do recall that outside the door, a little way down the street, there is a pipe that sticks out of the ground and people can turn the faucet on and wash their feet in summer.

My husband wondered why I didn't seem worried about the storm, how I could sit there rubbing the dogs' ears when he couldn't stop watching the reports or going to survival websites. He went shopping again and bought three new flashlights and a kayak paddle. After that, he got out his camera and took photos of the house to record how it looked before the storm came. He took a picture of me and it's the last one. I'm standing against the back wall of the house because I believed I could feel the ocean coming. I wanted communion with it, to feel the vibrations in the wood, the hum in the frame of the house as it approached. Out on the bay, the sky plowed the water and made it tilt and froth. Whitecaps merged— the white containing everything contained nothing. I was momentarily fearful and perhaps it was then that I sat in the car and tried to turn the engine on while the wind blasted, which was like sitting in the mouth of a lion. My husband was not in the car with me, but he was somewhere. I don't think the dogs, wherever they were, made a sound, though it's possible I wouldn't have heard it.

When the water came, it swallowed me and then I swallowed it. Conversion was a struggle between me and the person I had mistaken for me. Bubbles rushed, sparkling, to the surface. They hustled away limitations and boundaries, and at times I seemed to be the ocean. Not simply a creature within it, particulate and divided, but occupying a wholeness indescribably deep. Whatever happens on the surface doesn't find its way down. The darkest parts have the cool of a long-acquired stillness.

On the other hand, I watch my husband and Estelle. She has long legs and a ruby toe ring on her left foot. She has the worst laugh I have ever heard. The sound chops at the air until I realize the pressure in the room is revulsion and I want to make her stop it. You wonder at your own power even when you belong to nothing. The rage, white as a flame, is delicious and murderous—it snaps through the house and makes the dogs growl. I consider its fatal potentialities, but it subsides—the life of the animate is much too short. He stops her himself with his own body. Then I can't tell them apart, and there is the four p.m. light coming through the front windows, and I wonder when the room was painted.

―――――――

The second time that we lived here, the body of a sperm whale turned up on the beach and it was scored with gashes. The newspaper said it was a pygmy or a dwarf, that its demise was age-related, that it surfed in already dead. I assumed that its stunted growth was the fault of us all—the fishing nets and rubber ducks, petroleum and antidepressants. The skull was removed for keeping, a rib sent on to a lab and the rest buried ten feet deep into the sand. My husband and I went to stand beside the grave, which was carefully packed and evidence of a vigilance that had dragged its feet. I imagined people at the burial in dark clothing, a priest, maybe even a brass band and a second-line.

"I want to come back as a blue whale," my husband said. "Imagine having a heart the size of a car."

Down the road, the house that belonged to Estelle and her husband was white and blistered, and therefore almost invisible. Shortly after the appearance of the pygmy whale, she brought over a cake and her husband. I watched her slicing and serving, and was held in the grip of a sinister idea; I declined the cake, but eventually took the husband. Call him Ezra. I know that we were familiar because I remember a mole, like a tiny strawberry, on his right buttock. Also, their front door had a stickiness, as if it didn't want you to come or go. I remember wanting to go. There was a sky on the other side of the door that I suddenly needed to see and, moreover, there was the water. I had been plagued recently by aqueous dreams, full of kelp forests and filtered light. I felt that I might have the heart of a whale. I don't think I told my husband, but maybe I did. Or maybe Estelle marched over to say what we had done. Maybe she marched over and then she decided to stay. The sky was inordinately blue before the storm arrived, before it turned ash and pea gravel and sent down arms as dark as soil.

––––––––––

I sat inside the car, turning the key and listening to the engine as it struggled. I'm not sure where I thought I was going. There was more rain than anyone could remember, and it beat the roof of the car and blurred the windows. The engine turned on long enough for me to hear the radio announcer say, *"—important!"* I wanted to tell him that we had misunderstood, that our comings and goings mattered not at all. I pictured Virginia wading, with her stone-lined pockets, into the River Ouse. Madness had found her yet again, in Sussex; she had heard voices. I felt no such anguish, only the dropping away of names and a lightness I had once mistaken for fragility. The engine stopped again. I'm not sure where my husband was. The wind drove the ocean up past the beaches and the breakwalls.

*   *   *

The weather forecaster said that part of what made the storm so powerful was the rotation of the Earth itself, the Coriolis force. The jet stream didn't move in its usual pattern, but drew the hurricane toward shore where it joined a weaker system and gorged on the too-warm Atlantic. After twenty-four hours, the hurricane measured one thousand miles across and there was no hope in its eye. Hidden in the clouds, the moon turned full and hauled the ocean, folding it incessantly against the beaches. I felt the sea reveling in its new momentum as I watched the weather reporters blasted sideways, clutching light poles or their hats. Somewhere in the distance cars jammed roads that were vanishing.

I didn't have to convince my husband that we should stay, though we had different reasons. He didn't like the idea of water breeching its normal limits. "It's like a police force," he said, "that bursts into your home to search all the closets and drawers, every crevice, and you can't stop it. They leave it a wreck." He tugged at his hair. "It's like social media. It doesn't stop to rest." This reminded him to tweet our location, our condition, but everyone else was doing the same. My own condition was that I could feel the sea in my chest, how it filled my lungs and I could breathe, even better than before. I felt expansion, a capacity to run anywhere. He said to me, "Don't make a metaphor out of water. You don't know what you're doing." Not long after that, we finally dragged the plywood from the shed to cover the windows and I drove a hammer onto the heads of nails.

The tip of the water advanced hypnotically. It curled and bent. I had decided to face it wearing a nightgown and rubber boots, then added jeans under the nightgown and a sweatshirt on top. I remember that I took a wool hat, navy blue, the color of the sea before the storm, but I don't know what happened to it.

I staggered through the wind and got in the car again, because I had second thoughts and because the ground was still visible. I started the engine, which was soundless in the roar. I shut it off and got out. My husband called my name, or I think he did, but I couldn't see him. Further down the coast, the wind detonated beaches, roads, houses, but it was the ocean—no longer the ocean, but something else—that came to us. It is a trick of the eye that the first edge of water seems low and slow, like you're on the shore about to dip your feet. But then the ebb doesn't happen. I stood on the porch and waited for the water. It was a beautiful silver throat that swallowed everything.

My husband has rearranged the house, presumably to move on, but he keeps some newspaper clippings from the day of the sea. I saw them on a desk in a far corner of the bedroom. There is even a photograph that shows part of our house. I recognized the front door, the part that wasn't submerged, and the windows right away. Another photograph shows a house up the road. The house looks completely normal, except for being bathed in water, and it is similar to ours. Firemen are clustered along the edge of what would have been the porch if you could see it, up to their hips in water. They have their hands on the edge of a canoe and are helping a couple and their cat get into it. The funny thing about the picture is that the couple doesn't look the least bit concerned, even though they are getting ready to ride down the river that yesterday was their street.

part III

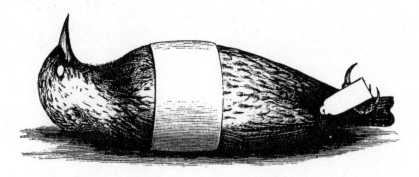

Part II

FIG. 25.—STARLING PROPERLY MADE INTO A SKIN WITH LABEL ATTACHED.

This, the arriving or newly-arrived birds hear, and, imagining it
proceeds from the throat of one of their species, who, entirely at his
ease, is letting the ornithological world know how excessively overjoyed
he is at his safe arrival, alight in the trees which surround and conceal
the treacherous imitator, and quickly fall a prey to the ready gun.
So infatuated are they, that enormous quantities are killed by this
method early in the season; in fact, I knew of one person who shot
one hundred and four, besides other birds, to his own gun in one day.

—MONTAGU BROWNE, *PRACTICAL TAXIDERMY*

CAPTIVITY

When the doctor gave me a pen and asked me to write down the crux of my problem, this was my response:

She had slept one hundred years—which is always the way it seems—one hundred years and the people she knew had lived and died, there had been wars and famines here and there, and kingdoms that were born and thrived and others that dissolved away, and still more that exploded, leaving rubble, and diseases that spread. Yet the world she woke to was verdant and the air was clear and the nurses, who were descended from her original coterie of caregivers, gave her plums that left stains on her fingers and cool glasses of water and took her, once she was able to stand, for slow walks in the institution's gardens. She learned her name, because she had forgotten it, and because her old clothes had been lost in a great fire, she was given some suitable clothing, some papers, and a bundle of money wrapped tight in rubber bands. Someone took her to the shining gates of the rebuilt institution, patted her shoulder, and told her, "Off you go now." When she turned to say thank you, nothing was there but a terrible field of ladies' mantle.

II

His disbelief is not explicit but I know it's there. I can't acknowledge what he hasn't said, but I'm a master of waiting. The chair is comfortable and there is a blanket, but it's on the other side of the room and neither of us has ever mentioned it. I never reach for his tissues or talk about the sadness of leaving one institution only to enter another. He asks me about my parents and I tell him about the day outside, or he asks about my childhood and I tell him about the Keepers. I tell him about sleeping, about being put to sleep, about being Sustained.

When I do that, he gives every impression of listening. Cocks his head and drinks me in, a little like a lover, if I didn't know better. If I didn't already know that he is filing his reports and making his guesses and assessments. He is kind in his disbelief, he tries to appear neutral. The bland eyebrow, the nonjudgmental mouth.

"One hundred years," he says, repeating what I've told him, handing the words back to me so I'll understand their unlikelihood. I don't mention that one of the other patients finds my story credible, except for one piece. "You're not beautiful. At all. Sleeping Beauty is *supposed* to be a beauty." He wants everyone to call him Napoleon—and who am I to argue?—and nearly stamped his foot. His feet were bare and his toenails covered in a fungus. Otherwise his appearance is generally tidy and he combs his hair while gazing into the reflection from the steel that frames the small windows.

I suppose Napoleon's assessment is correct. There is my large proboscis, and the unruly hair, currently shorn to eradicate the bedhead. The halitosis, still a little tenacious after the Sleep. There will always be someone who finds you beautiful, however, but I know how I look. If you sleep for one hundred years, you will find that upon waking the concepts of ugly and beautiful collide. The face that leans in toward you as you arrive at the surface will be a mix of pores and shiny skin and broken blood vessels. And then there it will be: the surprise of the irises.

I can't seem to stop moving, even if it's just to drum my fingers. The doctor tells me I have a condition though he doesn't name it. He says, "How were you put to sleep exactly?" and I know by his use of the word *exactly* that he is doubtful and doesn't like the answer that I've given numerous times already. I tell him it was a curse. As I slipped under, there was commotion, the smell of orange trees in the courtyard, and my mother yelling to shut the fortress doors. Beyond that, the vagaries of time in that other place. He says, "What other place? Where did you go?" and I say, "Where do you go when you sleep?"

I tell him about the images in my head, one hundred years of snips and halves and ghosts and pieces. Nothing I could describe well without becoming abstract. So he asks me, "What do you like about being abstract?" And how am I supposed to answer that?

One hundred years is enough time in which to shed your associations, even familial ones. I am no longer a daughter, a sister, a niece. Once upon a time, I tell him, and he stops me.

———————

While asleep I was raped by a man-ogre who tended my room, and I gave birth to twins who I'm told had tufts of hair in their ears. Their first drawings were given to me when I woke, though the twins and their father had passed on decades before—the ogre lifespan being extraordinarily short. I show the doctor the drawings, nearly identical depictions of giant headless mice by the children I never knew, and he says, "May I keep these?"

Perhaps waking is something that occurs in stages. There is a feeling to each level of consciousness that has more clarity than the one before, and so I have thought: *Yes, I am awake now*, only to find myself saying at some later point: *Now! I am awake!*

★　　★　　★

I tell him that occasionally I wonder if he really exists and if perhaps I'm still asleep, dreaming him. He uncrosses his legs and then crosses them again in the other direction. I suggest that I could give him a little more hair perhaps or stronger abdominal muscles. He suggests I tell him again about the moment I woke, what did I most want to do? I wanted to put my feet inside a pair of slippers—only that. I also wanted to get up and somehow know how to walk, and then to run. I say, instead, that I wanted to engage in sexual intercourse, and he writes that down, except that he writes more than that because he goes on writing for too long.

He suggests a kind of pill for my insomnia. When I fall asleep, I burst awake only moments later. Sometimes I can't control when and where I fall asleep but sleep rarely occurs when I want it to. I sprinkle lavender from the hospital's garden on my bed, drink milk, meditate. Masturbate. All gestures meant to mollify the idea of sleep without actually inducing it. Keep your pills, I tell him. He writes that down, with a Montblanc pen. When I comment on the pen, that's what he tells me: "Montblanc Starwalker Red Gold Metal Ballpoint." I say, "See there. An uncanny technological advancement." He looks up from his notebook.

"Many things must have changed since you were last awake," he says. "Anything surprise you?"

I tell him that I'm surprised that cars do not fly, not even a little, that religious and totalitarian regimes are still plentiful, and that he uses a pen. Why not a computer? I understand that his question is a tease and a kind of acquiescence at once, that he is trying to give me a small gift and at the same time chastise me for lying. I try to explain again that time is layered and nonlinear, it is a layer cake that can be sliced. You can touch whatever part of the cake you like and it will spring back to its original shape, as if, I tell him, you hadn't touched it at all.

It rains lightly and a nurse brings me outside so I can stand in the courtyard, which reminds me a little of the one from before, and feel the drops. I think I may never get used to them. Napoleon runs by, followed a moment later by a nurse. When the nurse walks him to the bench where I am sitting, he sits grumpily and flicks his long fingers repeatedly in the air. "She is not a Beauty!" he shrieks, and I take his hand and hold it gently. The veins in it are green and blue. He sits with me for an hour, longer than he has sat in one spot since coming to the hospital. When darkness arrives, he goes inside but I am allowed to stay where I am. I watch a tiny spider on the edge of the bench. Another moment arrives and everything, miraculously, is the same.

two stories
about
Glenn Gould

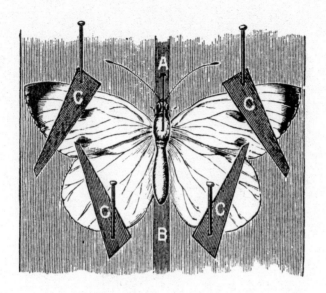

FIG. 48.—BUTTERFLY "BRACED" ON BOARD.

The larvae of moths and butterflies may be preserved by pressing
out the contents of their bodies, and by working from the head to
the tail in a gentle manner, and assisting the removal of the mass
by a careful dragging with a crochet needle. When empty, a little
corrosive sublimate solution may be injected with a metal or glass
blow-pipe, and the empty skin then distended by blowing into
it through a very fine blowpipe, made by drawing out in a clear
flame a small glass tube until it is attenuated to a fine point.

—MONTAGU BROWNE, *PRACTICAL TAXIDERMY*

LOON SEEKS MOTH

Wanted: Friendly, companionably reclusive, socially unacceptable, alcoholically abstemious, tirelessly talkative, zealously unjealous, spiritually intense, minimally turquoise, maximally ecstatic, loon seeks moth or moths with similar qualities for purposes of telephonic seduction, Tristanesque trip-taking and permanent flame-fluttering. No photos required, financial status immaterial, all ages and non-competitive vocations considered. Applicants should furnish cassette of sample conversation, notarized certification of marital disinclination, references re low-decibel vocal consistency, itineraries and sample receipts from previous, successfully completed out-of-town (moth) flights. All submissions treated confidentially, no paws need apply. Auditions for (all) promising candidates will be conducted to, and on, Avalon Peninsula, Nfld.

—GLENN GOULD'S UNPUBLISHED PERSONAL AD,
WRITTEN IN 1977 AND FOUND AFTER HIS DEATH

Dear Mr. Gould (Loon),

Death hardly matters! At least in this instance. I was fairly young when you died suddenly of a stroke—October 4, 1982. I remember the day because my father, who had all of your recordings—and there were a lot of them—wore black for three weeks afterward until my mother threatened to leave him. Years later he confided to me that his love for the cat was the real reason he started wearing his usual clothes again (the assumption here seems to be that my mother would have retained custody, which is likely, given that she once knitted matching vests for herself and Georgette). I bring this up only as an example of the tenuousness, and oddity, of many partnerships, even ones with a long track record and progeny (I was an only child, I should point out, as you were, and this is only one of numerous points of connection between us).

In matters of love, many people seem sure of being guided by higher powers, by meaning(!), but given the abysmal rate of successful matches, it would seem prudent to believe in a series of gambles, a single instance of which may pay off in the end, *if one is lucky*. I think some absurdity

would work in the formula, too, which is why I was
attracted to your use of Loon and Moth. By combining two
different species, you have, I think, gotten to the essence:
real companionship has to rise above what is taboo, and even
above the laws of nature.

I have never been referred to as Moth, but a little
research turned up some interesting, and coincidental, traits.
Many moths are nocturnal, a fact which you likely knew in
picking this creature as representative of your amour and
reflective of your own nighttime habits. I am an insomniac!
Sleep and I are old enemies. We do battle at least once every
twenty-four hours and the struggle is often prolonged.
In case this sounds erotic, let me assure you it is merely
repetitive. How nice it would be to have a companion who
is also saucer-eyed when everyone else is asleep; we could
discuss what we are each reading, or you could play and
I would listen. I am not a fellow pianist, however, and my
comments would be unlikely to help you, but I am, so they
tell me, a good listener.

Are you aware that some moths are born without
mouthparts? The caterpillars themselves may gorge on
leaves and whatnot, then construct new selves in their silk
cocoons, only to emerge with wings, but no mouth! For
those moths, their sole purpose appears to be mating. I will
try to refrain from too much analysis here, though, like
you, I do enjoy pulling apart a good puzzle. It is noteworthy
that you were afraid of flying—and took the train or drove
to avoid doing so—and yet have employed two winged
creatures in your search for companionship. I was a little

concerned that loons might dine on insects, such as moths, but my research tells me that they prefer *aquatic* insects and larvae.

Perhaps there is a more symbolic, or codelike, aspect to your wording. If by Loon you mean not the common *Gavia immer*, but someone with a psychic imbalance (also common, actually), and if by Moth you really mean mother, then I think I understand you. I do know you had a habit of giving animal labels to your loved ones (your father was Possum, your mother was Mouse, you were Spaniel), so perhaps you simply do mean Loon and Moth as they first appear. I have been accused of excessively mulling details, a habit I think you would appreciate.

You said you are unconcerned with financial status, but you would probably like to know the nature of my employment. I have worked for a number of years for the Secret Service. If you have been told that declaring that one works for the Secret Service is the same as saying that one doesn't, please don't believe it. And in case you think my admission indicates a lack of discretion, let me say that I regard secrets with great respect. I would not be able to tell you, for instance, the countries or government officials I have interacted with in my position, but I can divulge that my career has made me well suited to understanding the travail of a solitary existence, such as yours. We are both frequently misunderstood. We both have vocations that necessitate many hours of concentration and aloneness. Our careers sometimes require the jettisoning of superfluous others, including people for whom we have affection, but who sometimes get in the way of our goals. How I understand this! I've had to dispatch a person here and there.

I have spent a lot of time lurking, and watching, and trading in a few words for someone else's few words (these bits of information flying through the air are like music, and picking out the ones you need is like picking out the sound of the clarinet in a symphony), and I have waited ages for those signs of someone's comings and goings and reported on them—this has been my art (the difference between you and me is one of accolades, but that is the cost of a secret life). Our solitary existence, for the cause of art or spying, has given both of us an appreciation for the mechanical device as gatekeeper between ourselves and the world. You famously gave up live performances when you were only thirty-two, and devoted yourself to experimenting with recordings and radio until your death. It will not surprise you that recording devices have a special place in my heart, given what I do. We both love those technologies that can syphon from apparent emptiness tangible grains of information and shoot them into an eye or an ear. Your pianos do this, too, of course, they translate and amplify the musical idea in your head. You interpret the music, the piano interprets you. See? I get it, I really do.

You mentioned telephonic seduction, and I have to wonder if there is any better kind. In going over some of your papers, I did see that your telephone bills ran to the thousands of dollars, which is a great testimony to your conversational abilities. You would be relieved then that nowadays long-distance telephoning tends not to be as expensive as it once was, especially if one is using a landline, which are becoming rarer by the minute, and that I carry not one but three mobile phones on me at all times. (The cost of data is another matter, however, and I doubt that you would care for the text message, because of its inherent brevity.)

I have listened in on thousands of telephone calls, and been witness to thousands more unfettered transactions between humans. I have, during the time of my employment, observed many lovers, some of whom were also spies and adept at subterfuge, disguises, and misinformation. It has been enough to put me off the entanglements that are the norm and seek a Loon who might be seeking a Moth.

Apart from our convergences, there are areas where we diverge, I think, in complimentary ways. Love seems to function best with a mix of compatibility and tension if they occur in the proper ratio (a large region, for instance, of congeniality with a few pockets of disturbance, for a little spice, as it were). I have, for instance, a taxidermy hobby, and while I am aware of the incident when you were a child and had a fit regarding the catching of fish, you should know that I only practice taxidermy on creatures that I find already dead (typically in rural areas where my work sometimes takes me—you would be surprised at the number of safe houses and negotiation sites that exist down old country lanes) and never on fish (so far).

Where your music is concerned, I am, naturally, your biggest fan. So much so that in those discussions (which must bore you greatly now) about which is better, your earlier or later recording of the Goldberg Variations, I will break from my fellow combatants who choose one side vociferously over the other (to the point of fisticuffs) and tell you that I happen to enjoy them equally.

Lastly, as to location, I will happily *fly* anywhere for you. I have never been to Newfoundland, but I have been told it is a pretty place. I will bring my credentials and my notarized statement of disinclination to marry (and I can throw in an unwillingness to cohabitate, too, if you like). I will bring an old radio and we can use it to search for signs of life in the universe. Given that you are no longer alive yourself, you may be dwelling in a place without time, and arranging an exact moment of congress for the two of us could be difficult. On my side, I am governed by the rules of tangibility, its dimensions, its manifold clocks. Regardless of our obstacles, and the mysteries of how two people come together and eventually find themselves to be compatible, I do look forward to our meeting. I am writing this at 3:20 a.m. and think you will appreciate the lateness of the hour.

Yours truly,

(Luna) Moth

FIG. 23.—Skin of Bird turned ready for Severance from Body.

He added, too, the dangers of his lengthened journey, themselves no fiction; what seas, what lands he had beneath him from on high, and what stars he had reached with his waving wings.

—OVID, *METAMORPHOSES*

VERY OLD, ENORMOUS

Perhaps he had been struck by lightning; perhaps he had been reading
Márquez or the people watching had. He lay, or his body lay, by
the edge of a sea that, the day before, had boiled up so that there
had been no difference between the water and the sky. People
came at the start of the storm to see the surf shouldering up on
the land and one or two of them were pulled out in the currents,
folded in like raisins in cake batter. Now the winds and rain were
gone and coils of red line littered the beach, and there were the
pink tassels of a tricycle, a blue bottle, an ottoman. Gulls circled
and bawled above some crabs that had washed unluckily in. The
man was dug, black and seaweed-strewn, into the sand. His terrible wings were a collapsing tent that hid his body until a gust

came along and rolled him over. Children scurried to his side and poked him with sticks. They shrieked to their parents and then the parents shrieked and hid their children in their cars. Some men stood over him and nudged him with their feet, saying nothing. Nothing met his ears except the water frothing in and the gulls' cries and the breathing of the men.

Perhaps he had been struck by lightning, though he recalled nothing about it. He still wore his black coat and woolen scarf, which were shredded, but he could see that his feet were bare under the tangles of kelp and sand. His wings were unbroken, but even from his poor vantage he could tell they were a mess, the feathers thinned and blackened like a forest after a fire. One of the men kicked him in the ribs, and he felt hands clamping various parts of him. Half dead, or fully dead, he was heavy. He was powerless to help them help him up. Nothing he could do but give in to their rotations and grapplings while they tried to right him. He heard curse words and someone said, "What an old buzzard. Jesus. Look at those wings." Where the men's hands were not crowding him, he felt the breadth of the sky all around, it was still grey and clotted with rain clouds that were moving speedily away and why wasn't he within them? He felt a knee indecorously in his ass, some fingers in his ribs, and his own weight sinking into their grasp as the men remarked on his size and cursed him for not helping. His wings beat feebly at their chests, scratched at the air and overcoats, and he shut his eyes to concentrate, but nothing. The sky retreated, smaller, unscalable. He clutched a bad face, his fingers in a furred nostril, an eye. He heard shrieking, either avian or human, as the sky wobbled away from him like a dropped saucer.

When he woke, he was in a large cage, and there were children again, but instead of sticks they prodded him with their fingers; one child had a putter. Beyond them his hosts moved smudgily as they talked about him without actually looking at him. He rubbed his eyes. The cage was situated in a backyard with a broken fence and a Cadillac chassis. A cockatoo with an ankle tether but otherwise open air watched him from a back porch piled high with lobster traps. His sensitive ears heard someone call the bird hey Bub, but hey Bub did nothing. He heard bottles being opened and a young man poured beer into a bowl for him and slid it cautiously through an opening at the floor of the cage. He tipped the bowl clumsily into his mouth, only because he was sure he was dying, making loud slurps, and heard laughter all around him.

A woman's face appeared at his cage. Perhaps she was fifty, maybe sixty. "Thirsty, are you? Have some more." He nudged the dish back through the opening and she filled it, smiling at him, and nudged it back. He turned away from her to drink it, hidden by the enormous wings. "My soul, but those are pathetic." She walked around the edge of the cage to look again at his face. Perhaps her expression was not unkind. He allowed her to stare.

"I suppose you'd like to know my name. It's Amelia. A-me-lia. Now maybe you'll say your name." She waited and looked him over, tilting her head, just like hey Bub. She smiled again and called over her shoulder, "Lorne! Come over here!"

Lorne was older than the woman and his eyes were wild

behind his glasses. He walked over cautiously, clutching a baseball bat. Amelia swiped her hand at him. "Settle down, fool."

Lorne set the tip of the bat on the ground and propped himself against it. "Well? What do you say?"

"Look at his face. Really look at it," she said, and Lorne leaned forward. "What do you think? Recognize him?"

He looked over his glasses at her. "He looks a little like Columbo."

"No! Don't you think he looks like that piano player? Glenn Gould?" She huffed air into her palms and rubbed her fingers as if to warm them. Before she married Lorne the fisherman she was married to Haruto the violinist. "He looks just like Glenn Gould."

Lorne looked at the man with enormous wings warily. After a while he said, "If you say so. I guess he resembles him a little."

"A little! He's exactly like the picture on the Goldberg Variations. The 1981 recording, when he's balding." She looked right into the man's heavily browed eyes and he stared back. She noted the mole above his lip. "Exactly."

He did not talk, but when Amelia and Lorne went away he hummed. One of the children, disliking the sound or wanting to make an offering of some kind, rummaged near the Cadillac chassis and dragged over a paint-splotched radio connected to twenty feet of extension cord. The girl set the radio in the dirt beside the cage and crouched by the dials. The man stopped humming and watched her, budging his sore bones, his still-wet clothes closer to the edge of the cage. A sound like bolts in a metal pipe emerged from the radio, and as the girl searched for live waves, she found more clashes that made the man shut his eyes with pleasure, until finally she settled on a spot between Beethoven's Sonata No. 1 in F Minor and Outkast's "Rosa Parks." Every few seconds the news: a man opened fire in a Laundromat, the DOW was up 815 points, people on a mountain were never found, but their names crackled contrapuntally in. The children watched the man, his head swaying. They leapt back when he raised his hand and pointed at the lawn mower. A boy said, "This?" He started the mower after three hard yanks and the man smiled, showing five teeth missing. There was something else he wanted: the leaf vacuum propped like a rifle against the shed. Another boy fired it up, unleashing a rabid sound. The old man waved him back until the boy stood closer to the back porch. He indicated to the girl to turn up the radio's volume, work the dials, the boy with the lawn mower to remain where he was. Amelia and Lorne came running out of the house to find the man in the cage rocking, eyes shut, his left hand appearing to conduct.

[Glenn Gould] I've always had some sort of intuition that for every hour that you spend in the company of other human beings you need X number of hours alone. Now, what that X represents I don't really know; it might be two and seven-eighths or seven and two-eighths, but it's a substantial ratio. Radio, in any case, is a medium I've been very close to ever since I was a child, that I listen to virtually nonstop: I mean, it's wallpaper for me—I sleep with the radio on, in fact now I'm incapable of sleeping *without* the radio on, ever since I gave up Nembutal [laughing].

[Jonathan Cott] *Does it affect your dreams?*

[Gould] Sure, in the sense that if there are newscasts on the hour, I pick up the bulletins and use them as the subjects for my dreams. In the morning, if there's been a boat that's just gone down, I'll think, "Gee, that was an odd dream about the *Titanic* I had last night," and then pick up the paper at the door: "*Lusitania* Sinks," and I will, of course, have concocted my own dream variation on the story already.*

Word got around that Glenn Gould was being held captive in the neighborhood. That he had been dead for some years bothered no one. There was a commemorative statue sitting bronzely outside the CBC studios in Toronto where he could finally be made to endure the touch of other people 24-7; but that was Toronto and another thing entirely. The people in the neighborhood turned up outside his cage to take pictures with their phones and see if he was, in fact, Gouldian. They asked him to sign their albums and CDs, offered him boxes of arrowroot biscuits, a few tried to get him to soak his hands in a tub of hot water placed beside the cage. One of the onlookers bellowed for no one to spread their germs to the man and spent hours mopping the bars with disinfectant and giving him bottles of water in place of the beer, because Gould had been known to drink Poland Spring.

On Wednesday people also turned up at the edge of the sea because a Steinway grand had washed in, gutted and stinking and

---

* From *Conversations with Glenn Gould* by Jonathan Cott

seeming to affirm the identity of the visitor. A music professor at the university was asked to investigate the winged man's authenticity, and in light of the additional find of the piano, which was in the process of being suctioned from the sand and brought to the house, the professor showed up with a folding bridge chair under his arm, a replica of Gould's preferred seating. Its back did not contain the silhouette of a leaf, nor had the height been lovingly rendered by a father, but the legs were shortened and amended with adjustable pieces of metal, like the original, so that whoever sat on it would find themselves able to flex and slouch only fourteen inches from the ground, rather than the usual twenty-give-or-take of a piano bench. The seat had also been altered to match the original so that most of it was missing except the outer rim and the middle crossbar. "We'll see how he sits," said the professor, holding in his mind the beautiful image of Gould curled at the keys, as Amelia served him rum punch and lobster rolls and he directed his words at her chest. "That will tell us a good deal."

Amelia and Lorne allowed the man to keep the radio beside the cage where he could use his wiry fingers to turn the dials. Much of the time he kept his head close to the speakers, and rarely turned his gaze to the people who now paid a fee to watch or film him, including the drunk who took out his member and pissed a stream of dehydrated amber through the rusting bars (the video of which showed the piss lit resplendently by the setting sun against the blackened depravity of the hunched, winged man, set to Orlando Gibbons's Fantasy in C Major, and which was viewed 578,344 times on the first day). Several women got the same idea to bring

him new overcoats and knitted scarves, despite the air temperature being somewhat balmy, but he seemed to prefer the ones he
already wore and the offerings remained untouched in a corner
until he decided to sit on them (another viral hit).

[Gould] I've never conceded any real contradiction between
the assumption that one can have a rather solitary existence
and the fact that one can supportively have radio in the back-
ground at all times. I mean, we talked last week about a purely
physical demonstration of its power—you know, its power to
block out mental impediments; we talked about Beethoven's
Opus 109. I'm totally incapable of understanding people who
get upset with any kind of Muzak. I can go up and down endless elevators and never be bothered by it. No matter how
insipid the stuff may be, I really don't care—I'm utterly un-
discriminating.**

The man watched as the battered Steinway grand was wheeled
sideways from the alley behind his cage and into the house by
several men, and then righted with much yelling. Finally, there
was quiet. The man could see through the open doors of the
back porch that the interior room had been cleared out and the
piano took up most of the space. But it was a salt-stained monster, cracked in places, festooned with seaweed and a dead gull
caught in a vascular tangle of line. Amelia came to his cage and
unlocked the door. Lorne stood behind her with his bat, just in

---

** From *Conversations with Glenn Gould* by Jonathan Cott

case. Between the man and the piano was a clear path, lined on either side with the neighbors. When he stepped out of the cage, he refused to look at the open sky that had earlier forsaken him and stepped unsteadily toward the piano. The spectators rocked in accordance with his direction, as he staggered forward with one wing twisted, and veered unpredictably. Even crouching he was taller than any of them and his wings when they twitched made the children scream. He shed scapular and tertiary feathers as his bare feet scraped the ground, clogging his toenails with more debris, until at last he hunched before the folding chair and the Steinway.

What did the people expect? Performance was a trap for the performer. Surely they knew that Glenn Gould had not given a concert since April 1964 in Los Angeles when he was a mere thirty-two. The oceanic piano was a bust; the hammer felts had been nibbled by sea creatures, the wood warped, the spruce soundboard glutted with water, the strings pulled and rusted by currents, and the interior iron plate was cracked as if the beast had been dropped long before it had ever found itself inside an ocean. None of the keys was missing, however, and the pedals remained intact, leading some who crowded around the piano to overlook the disastrous guts and expect to hear not only a sound, but actual music. The man touched the warped lid, which someone had propped open with a two-by-four, then looked down at the chair for a long moment before lowering himself carefully onto it and adjusting himself on the crossbar. Someone let out a shriek.

*   *   *

Much as we want our talents in isolation, thought the man. When hardly a sound came from the piano or the man at all—only a muffle that could as easily have come from inside a closet two houses over—the crowd gaped. No Bach partitas or fugues, Beethoven sonatas, Gibbons or Byrde or Sweelinck, no humming. People hunched in disappointment, slouched for the doors. The music professor waved the old man from the chair, packed it up, and left. Hey Bub was put away in the kitchen.

Amelia, much as she had enjoyed the extra income, was relieved. An imposter Glenn Gould, she figured, was in the end better than the genuine article. She would have her yard back, her life. The piano returned to the sea. Perhaps she would hang laundry to dry on the cage or grow yellow roses up the sides of it. Lorne could put away his bat.

The man with enormous wings, however, did not take the hint, even when Lorne got out his tool kit and permanently removed the cage door. Lorne even shooed the man toward a hole in the fence large enough to fit him. He stuffed money and a fried clam sandwich into the coat's dulsey pockets and even gave the smelly man a little shove. "Go." Nothing. The man looked up at the sky, but there was only bright sun and offensive blue and not the grey he preferred. The sky, in fact, lacked the necessary particles, the texture for ascent. For the time being, at least, he was grounded.

[Cott] *Maybe your feelings about solitude come from the fact that you've got a Nordic temperament.*

[Gould] That certainly is part of it. It's an ambition of mine, which I never seem to get around to realizing, to spend at least one winter north of the Arctic Circle. Anyone can go there in the summer when the sun is up, but I want to go there when the sun is down, I really do, and so help me I'm going to do it one of these times. I've said this now for five or six years, and every year the schedule gets in the way.***

***

*** From *Conversations with Glenn Gould* by Jonathan Cott

The night's third portion come
when now the stars
Had travers'd the mid-sky, cloud-
gatherer Jove
Call'd forth a vehement wind
with tempest charged,
Menacing earth and sea with
pithy clouds
Tremendous, and the night fell
dark from heav'n.

—HOMER, *THE ODYSSEY*

MESSAGES FROM THE SNOW

Chatter.

1.

The messages began to arrive on Sasha's skin as the snow began to fall, somewhere in late November. She had been itching and lonely for weeks and contemplating messages in general, the ones—or lack of them—in her email and on her phone, how they travelled invisibly, most of them unbidden and unimportant. Words from someone, somewhere, out of nowhere, and rarely from the person she wished (though who, really, did she wish would communicate with her?). Perhaps receiving a message on her skin, on her own epidermis, was not more strange than receiving one on her phone. The outside world, it seemed, was bent on mumbling and hollering. The chief difference in this case being that she was in agreement that her phone and her computer should receive messages, but she had not agreed upon a similar arrangement for her skin. Especially one in which the message was hailed by violent and intractable itching.

2.

She was under a lot of stress, this was true. She had left her job as a social worker to care for her elderly mother, Oksana—not *Mom*, *Mama*, and definitely not ever, even when she, Dima, and Anna were children, *Mummy*—and so she and Oksana shared her small apartment in a high-rise that shed bits of its facade to the street below and had brightly lit but odorous hallways. Sometimes Dima, and occasionally Anna who lived further away in Jersey, took Oksana for errands or appointments, but they had children of their own, while Sasha did not, they often pointed out, and so . . . Oksana had begun to waver between lucidity and dementia and could no longer be left alone.

3.

Each message began the same way, a ferocious itch, somewhere—anywhere—on her body and a graphite cursive that surfaced, like a tiny tattoo, and peeled off easily in one strip, a substance between skin and paper. Vaguely glittering, translucent. A testimony to the body's weirdness, a hymn of its unseemliness.

The first message came inconveniently the last time she had sex with Marcus, which was a week ago.

No, go back further in that day. Before Marcus.

1.

Oksana was at Anna's house, so Sasha went to her volunteering gig at the food bank five blocks over from her apartment, shoving her way between the men from the methadone clinic who stood on the sidewalk. It was a matter of pride for her to show them she wasn't afraid, that she was small and sharp. For a few hours, she unboxed donations and inspected the tops and bottoms of cans, the seams of flour and sugar bags, she unscrewed the lids of peanut butter jars to make sure there was an inner seal. She worked alongside three women in large sweatshirts who cackled every so often and startled her. They called her Snow White, because she was so pale. One of them pressed her hand. Sasha plotted out the number of minutes before she could maneuver casually to the pantry sink and scrub her hands with the fluorescent soap that was supposed to smell like pomegranates. Everything they used at the pantry had been donated from somewhere; she herself had been known to bring in bags of soap and cleaners, until someone thought she was taking them instead of bringing. You never knew, the accusing man had said. He had a splotch on his forehead exactly like Gorbachev, and she said nothing in response, just stared at the island. She had been working beside the women for an hour when she felt the twinges again of an itch. Which would have been nothing if she had not been experiencing bouts of itching as wild as seizures for several days. "What, Snowy—you're leaving?" one of them cackled, as Sasha grabbed her coat and scarf and bolted for the exit.

2.

Hurrying toward her apartment she came across her neighbor Althea, and Althea's dog, a fifty-pound mixed breed named Shoe. Althea smiled at her as they got closer, but Shoe was ten feet ahead on his lead, straining, wearing a thick wool vest and a little leather hat. He was a snapper and a growler, but Althea pretended not to notice; in truth, she liked the effect of letting the lead out in such a way that Shoe came within inches of a target but not close enough to actually do any damage. She smiled even wider at Sasha. "Sure is cold, isn't it? Another storm coming . . ."

"Okay, okay," Sasha murmured as she stepped her rubber boot into the slush to avoid Shoe. She flailed with an itch, a spastic shimmer of her arms sudden enough for Shoe to yelp as if stung. Althea yanked hard on his lead and scowled at Sasha, "What'd you do? What'd you do to him?"

Sasha stumbled on, scrambling over the chunky ice and debris of the sidewalks and half laughing, snorting. She jammed her knit hat over her hair, which lately had been turning more grey, and tried to fit her fingers inside her coat sleeve to scratch. Outside her apartment building there was a large divot in the pavement filled with street water. She had the urge to fling herself into it and feel the freezing sludge short-circuit the itch.

3.

The itch sprouted on top of her ribs. She made three frantic attempts at the code to enter her building, then once inside her own foyer and certain that Oksana had not returned, she flung off her coat, tore off her sweater, and saw her bra-clad image in the mirror, a terrible itch-ridden guffaw on her face. She could have counted her ribs, easily, if she were not busy scratching. She panted and pulled her fingertips away from her ribs, felt the particles and nerve endings twinge and fire up, and she scratched again. It occurred to her that a joint would help, the heat and comfort of the first draw. She scrambled to the kitchen cupboards, still scratching, found the one she had rolled two weeks earlier tucked behind the flour and the black beans, and she managed to light it with one hand.

4.

The joint, the fleeting experience of ecstasy, and the fact that her mother wasn't in the apartment, as well as a desire to distract herself from the itching, all contributed to her letting Marcus in when he knocked at her door. He lived three floors above and was one of five owners (all of whom went to film school together two decades before) of a restaurant that served its clientele in the dark; they were a surprise sellout each night, and Marcus had taken on the habit of squinting and feeling everything with his hands. He said he was gaining sensitivities and proclivities where none had existed; he thought he was developing supersonic hearing.

"Babe, put something on," he whispered and shut the door behind him.

5.

It was a relationship surely in its last days, but for five minutes she was more relaxed than she had been in months. The itch was still present, however, having settled like a leech on her shoulder and causing her to utter sounds that Marcus interpreted as sexual praise. He breathed into her neck, exactly on the spot that itched, and she writhed in a way that surprised and delighted him. Then he said, "What is *that*?" noticing not just that her skin was red, but that it seemed to bloodlessly lift. There was an edge.

"What do you mean?" she said, and touched the spot with her fingertips. She felt something catch, and it was papery and sharp. She pushed him away and sat up. What, indeed. The itch was suddenly gone from her shoulder, but something was there in its spot, a piece of molting skin. She pinched her index finger and thumb together along one edge of it and pulled. A ripping sound, like

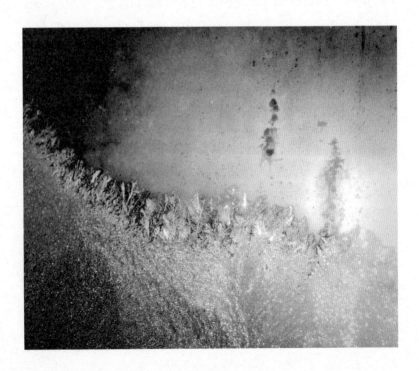

paper, and it came away painlessly. She squinted to make out the letters that were tiny and messily written, apparently in pencil.

Flummoxed, Marcus simply said, "What does it say?"

She folded the tiny paper twice so that it measured only a centimeter.

"Nothing," she said, and pulled the blanket around her.

Sweet nothings.

1.

The first message said,

> *Testing.*

2.

This was followed an hour later (and forty-five minutes after Marcus had left) by

> *Ominous black flag*

which was followed shortly thereafter by

> *The surface undulates considerably about this latitude;*

and

> *Weather very curious, snow clouds,*

Clearly the pot she had smoked was either first-rate or grievously engineered. The first message ended up momentarily in the waste bin, until she retrieved it, flattened it out, and hid it inside her day planner. She stared at the other two, shone a flashlight through their translucence, wondered briefly that her body had produced such a thing—though she did not feel any particular reverence, despite her ongoing loneliness, for the notion that someone somewhere was communicating with her—before hastily fitting them into her planner with the first.

3.

She stood in the tub and examined her naked body for other oddities, yet she didn't want to look too closely. Taking up the scissors that rested on the tub's edge, she peered into a plastic mirror suctioned to the tile. She was accustomed to cutting her own hair, which she kept short and tweaked up with paste, especially when she was disturbed about something. She made a few snips and the hairs fell delicately, in teeny clumps, feathery and dark against the white. For a moment she was itchless. Her muscles were tight, as if strung with piano wire, and a few poles tented up the skin in places. She had not been hungry for several weeks and perhaps had lost a few pounds.

She climbed out of the tub and examined her leg where another tab had lifted.

We pick up four days' food.

From her left breast, she peeled,

It was blowing quite hard and drifting

The feeling of the papers as they fell away was curious, almost as subtle as stray hairs falling. She could not detect a pattern in timing, though perhaps it was too soon. Oksana was due back within the hour. The next ones came with more scratching and agitation in quick succession:

I think Oates is feeling the cold and fatigue more than most of us.

Awoke to a stiff blizzard;

but, by Jove! It has been a grind.

All from her right inner thigh. These, too, she collected, smoothed out, and placed in the planner.

4.

When she saw the name Oates, she understood if not the why or the how, then the provenance. Her father, dead five years, had in his last months an acute fascination for the doomed polar expedition (though she could not have said which pole) of Robert Falcon Scott. Oates, she recalled, was the man who went out into the storm to die, or some such thing that her father had gone on about and to which she had paid only enough attention to be mildly annoyed.

Oksana comes home.

1.

Anna, her dark hair combed carefully back and with a parka over her suit, brought Oksana back and promptly left—she had a case to prepare that involved a café overrun with baby strollers—by which point Sasha had covered her skin in lotion in the hope of sticking down any messages about to release and gotten dressed. Oksana stood on the rubber mat at the door and worked at her coat, peeling each button slowly before becoming lost in sniffing the air. Her sense of smell had left her and caused both cheese and chocolate to taste of chalk, but she insisted otherwise. Sasha pretended to concentrate on helping her.

"You don't fool me. I have the nose of a—what are the ones that hunt truffles?" Briefly, everything was leaf mould and forest floor.

"Pigs?"

"You made coffee."

"Yes, but it's all gone," Sasha said. "I did get you bagels, though. And not the marble kind, which you don't like."

"Too bad. Marbles are beautiful." Oksana sat in the chair that Sasha kept beside the front door so she could take off her boots, and huffed. "You know what your nephew said to me?"

"Which one?" Sasha knelt and untied the laces. The boots were enormous on the nodular feet covered by two pairs of wool socks, hunter orange.

"The cross-eyed one. Daniel? Edgar?"

"Matty. I'm not sure where you got Edgar."

"Huh. Sure enough."

"So what did he say?"

"He said, 'If you keep a goldfish in the dark, it will turn pale.' I've been repeating it so I'd remember to tell you." She watched Sasha undoing the knot. What she wanted more than bagels was the tiny flask hidden in her deep sweater pocket and the nub of a fat cigar that she never lit but liked to smell—it was the only thing that got through—and that was nestled in a tissue inside her purse. "It seemed important at the time."

2.

Oksana liked to be bathed, to feel the water coast down her bare back, to sit there even as the temperature cooled. Sasha sometimes would have to beg her to get out. Oksana leaned into the faucet and laughed at her distorted face in the reflection. "An eagle," she said. "Wondrous animal." The conflations of old age amazed her, the metamorphoses. Each day was a new creature.

Sasha covered her mother's spine with a trail of foam and said, "An eagle? What do you mean?"

"It's a fucking eagle. That's all I know." It was gone and Oksana's face relaxed again. She smiled at Sasha, water rolling in beads over her breasts and the folds of her stomach. She stared at Sasha's arm where a paper was starting to lift, enticing and glinty as a fish scale.

Sasha saw astonishment flash over her mother's face and she drew her arm back, but not quickly enough. Oksana could be fast, surprisingly so. In spite of mobility issues and nerves that would unpredictably fire or not, she could still dart into traffic as fast as a cat, she could snatch food from another person's plate and gulp it down almost in one gesture. She pinched the little tab from Sasha's arm into her mouth and swallowed before Sasha could protest.

full blizzard at lunch,

Oksana grinned and threw her head back to laugh, her scalp bright pink and glowing under the sparse white hair.

Sasha said, "Did you even look at it?"

"I'm sorry. I'm sorry." She laughed again and hid her face with her fingers, then slid them down so they rested contentedly on her stomach. Sasha thought she looked like the little carved Buddha that sat on the dash of her dealer's car.

A serious look came over Oksana's face. "I saw John F. Kennedy that one time. You remember? His face was like the sun. Tuesday."

"I know. You've told me about it. But it wasn't Tuesday, it was over fifty years ago."

"You could fry an egg on it. He was so beautiful."

Sasha handed her mother a washcloth. "You liked his tie."

"I liked all of him."

Sasha snorted. "Honestly."

"I'm old. I can say what I please." Oksana watched her hands in the water, the bone knobs. "I could die tonight, you know." The invisible world rose up in her mind. She could hear Bach's Quartet in B-Flat Major inside her skull, she saw the depth of stars inside the chocolate pudding that Sasha made for her last night, a nebula birthing a star right there in the mound of her spoon. But no point in mentioning. The images and sounds usu-

ally flickered out as soon as appearing, almost the same moment. She wanted to say to Sasha that she would find it out
eventually, when her own joints throbbed up, but the words
were never quite there, not entirely decent. Sometimes she
would open her mouth and unintended profanities would burst
out, even though she had spent eight decades with speech so
clean the nuns at St. Margaret's could have laid out the sacra-
ment on it, the bitches.

3.

"You're too thin. I don't like too thin," Oksana said.

Sasha soaped her mother's back again and it was one time too
many. Oksana grabbed the sponge and bit it; the joke she was
making was hilarious and nuanced, if only Sasha would pay attention. But this was the way it was with offspring. You got what
you got. They grew up and one day the thought arrived that they
were nothing like you, had nothing to do with you, even if they
stood in the same room, exchanging the same dust particles in
their lungs. The problem with Sasha was a lack of humor, and
really the world was so funny, especially when viewed from the
tub.

"I could die tonight," she said.

Sasha said nothing for a moment, but arranged the little
figurines, two rabbits, a frog, three cherubic children, that had
once sat on the bookshelves of her childhood home; when Oksana moved in, she put them in a row above the toilet, saying,
"I should throw them out, but I can't do it. It's because they're
ugly."

4.

Sasha believed it was Oksana's greatest wish to die during the night, "cheap and easy." She puffed up her cheeks, and said, "I don't know. I don't know. I hope not. I don't think you should say it every night."

"Because Santa is listening . . ." Oksana said.

Sasha sighed and got a towel from the closet. She felt a cluster of words flutter down inside her pant leg, soft as spiders. She pushed them away with her foot, hoping that her mother would not notice. Oksana peered over the edge of the tub, however, as if she were hanging over the gunwales of the ship that bore her, age five, across the Atlantic, a Russian Jew who would end up in a Catholic orphanage. The papers had been wrong, or miss-stamped, or water soaked, and by the time the error was sorted out, three years had gone by and it was considered prudent to let her stay. With the bitches, Oksana would clarify.

"Skin tags," she said.

"What?"

"Skin tags. You have skin tags."

"I hadn't thought what to call them," Sasha said, looking at how they curled in the humidity, almost luminous.

The old tracks show so remarkably well

—a great piece of luck.

Forty-five miles to the next depot and six days' food in hand.

"I'm going to be a bad boyfriend and look at them later. Are you ready to get out?"

"The eagle has landed. Give me the fucking saxophone."

Sasha helped her to stand and gave her the towel. Her mother, who had been complaining of shrinking, seemed almost towering.

Perseverance.

1.

As she sat on the bed, Sasha arranged the messages in front of her, including the latest ones.

a spatter of hard snow-flicks where feet had trodden.

We are getting more hungry, there is no doubt.

The lunch meal is beginning to seem inadequate.

She did not care for the content and would have preferred them, if anything, to be blank. If she was speaking of choices and aesthetics and her own personal concerns. She was mesmerized by how they fell, however, the feeling as they sloughed off. They landed with a little tick, uncannily like a clock. If she had a say in the matter, and apparently she did not, the papers would be little voids that fell, little nothings. Or they would not fall at all. They would not exist. She worried that they frightened Oksana, although she had to concede that this seemed unlikely, as her mother's two settings were annoyance or amusement.

2.

She did not sense, exactly, the explorer coming through her skin. The words felt like an echo and she did not believe in ghosts. What people took for ghosts was really their own fear projected outward. Nor did she think that it was her father who was sending messages from beyond. They had not been close, and though she thought of him occasionally, she rarely cried about his death. She doubted, too, that he—wherever he was—ever cried about her. They had not been that kind of family. It was the physical aspect of her situation that concerned her, whether or not it would end, the terrible itchiness, and how she would continue to manage out in the world, shedding and disseminating and peeling wherever she went, a reluctant conduit for whatever it was on the other end. Surely her unwillingness should count. Her resistance would create, she hoped sooner rather than later, an obstruction to the words coming through. She vowed to slather on more lotion and double up her sweaters.

3.

A message released from the back of her neck,

the conditions are more favourable.

She let out a little cry of frustration and hoped that Oksana could not hear her.

———

Oksana dreams of death.

1.

That night Oksana had dreams about dark pools in which her husband was swimming. He had been as thin and mild as a stick insect and just as awkward. Moments later, his dream heart, small, still beating, was there in her hands.

2.

She often dreamed about his last days. He had asked her to suffocate him or overmedicate him or do whatever it took to bring an end to his suffering. Instead, she had compressed the idea of his death into a hard splinter and drove it over and over into his heart, during the nights as she tried to sleep, as she shook his pills into a cup, as she soaped the dinner plates. Eventually she sensed a shift, as if Death were a creature who suddenly detected they were there, turned, and looked at them.

On a drizzly Saturday, they stood on a little bridge in the park, and her husband abandoned his walker to leap up onto the railing as lithe as a panther, and as dark, in his black overcoat. He hunched there in the rain and Oksana held her breath, unsure of what was happening, until she saw him dive gracefully—the only smooth curve he had ever made—into the air beside the bridge, and fall a short distance into the water below—a distance that was not enough to kill a person. The autopsy would reveal that he had gone into cardiac arrest. "At last," she said, looking over the railing, her husband only fifteen feet down, a black coil inside the lapping pond water.

3.

She woke late in the morning with unusual clarity. She woke with envy, desires, fascinations that were crystalline. She knew unequivocally who she was. She remembered that her husband was dead, the names of her children, that she lived with Sasha. And she knew that Sasha received messages on her skin, and who they were from, because she had snuck into Sasha's room and saw them arranged on the bedspread. She had recognized the predicament in them immediately, the polar calamity. Nothing was new, and either everything was strange, or nothing was.

4.

Sasha made her a soup and sandwich for lunch and Oksana sat at their tiny dining table and ate it. She watched her daughter, who had just returned from going down the block for Oksana's favorite crackers, as she brushed the snow from her coat and shook out her hat. Oksana felt a ripple of jealousy as she sipped at her tomato soup. The problem with living in this apartment, she felt, was that she could not go out in the snow—and there had been more snow recently than other years—whenever she wanted. People, Sasha included, did not realize what a miracle snow was, how profligate. An elaboration so absurd and breathtaking; also, misunderstood for being commonplace. She wanted a lightness, and a ferocity, like snow. To move in the mode of a storm. To be outside in the air and not subject to the recycled stuffing of the apartment. The huffings and sighings of so many strange people, mingling in the vents.

Theatre of the mind.

1.

She spent an hour convincing Sasha of her lucidity and that they should go out. When Sasha looked at her doubtfully and said, "Where," Oksana suggested they see a play, that they should spring for third-row seats at an Off-Broadway matinee. It was occurring to her that all their frugality was somewhat excessive, it had been so long since she had been to the theatre, and miraculously Sasha agreed and found tickets online. Even though the snow was falling, Sasha got a cab easily and helped her mother in. They soon found themselves at the theatre, wedged into seats between men on either side whose arms and knees bulged. When the lights dimmed, however, Oksana felt cozy, fixed in her seat with the velvety dark all around and the snow bashing the hell out of things outside. Oh, but the snow. She had almost opened her mouth to catch some of the flakes as they were getting into the cab, but thought better of it. She well knew that Sasha embarrassed easily and they had already exchanged words because Oksana refused to bring her cane. The problem with the cane was not that it was unhelpful, but that it was a tin line with a black rubber tip that hyphenated the space between her and the ground. It said she was a heaviness that needed propping up. It said: The End. Oh, but never mind, there was the snow. The lightness she wanted, the freedom, and if she looked deeper, she would find, too, a desire to cover, whitewash, obliterate whatever she chose.

2.

She felt Sasha reach over and remove the candy she was trying to work out of its wrapper. No matter, there was enough going on elsewhere. You never knew what would happen onstage, the chance of seeing the mistakes and goofs that flew out at the audience as black as bats. The missing prop, the forgotten line, the sour note. She adored it; it had been too long. There was the life and death struggle that somehow transmogrified into the real. She remembered—this was vivid—reading about the tenor, for instance, who died of a heart attack at the Met during a performance of *The Makropulos Case*. Right there onstage, 8:15 p.m., immediately after belting the line, "You can only live so long." Oh, to have been there. He had landed on his back, the *Times* said, arms outstretched. She had clipped the article, she enjoyed it so much. What did he know, and when? It was the ultimate gesture, she felt, a gift to the viewers to time it exactly so, though she imagined that the audience must have considered it part of the opera. Likely there was a bad moment when the counterfeit image revealed itself to be the genuine article.

"Imagine!" she said out loud to Sasha who shushed her, imagine being able to pull off such an exquisite exit. She hoped he had had one of those out-of-body experiences that were supposed to accompany people crossing over, that he had glimpsed himself sprawled there and the scurrying that would have overtaken his body, like ants piling on a crushed sandwich. *Bravo*, Oksana thought, *bravo*.

3.

She loved the play, which was *King Lear* with an exuberant old actor playing the lead, and they had been close enough to see the saliva arc from Lear's raging mouth into the stage lights. She thought it was wonderful to see such unbridled rants, an irascible man so unlike her husband. Even Sasha had seemed to enjoy herself, and now they strolled along the street, Oksana having convinced her that they did not need a taxi, which would be hard to get anyway, they could simply walk. Sasha was uneasy, as the snow that hit the sidewalks began to stick in places. Most areas had been salted already, however, and she sensed that her mother was present, she seemed to be herself today, and her feet were unusually steady as they walked.

4.

Sasha had agreed to see the play because she wanted to distract herself from the messages coming through. She put the ones that had unraveled during the play in her pocket,

Wilson's leg much better.

Evans' fingers now very bad, two nails coming off, blisters burst.

Just before lunch unexpectedly fell into crevasses,

and kept her hand ungloved so she could feel the strangeness of them, like onionskins and wasp nests. The benefit of her mother's cyclical memory was that she seemed not to recall that her daughter was receiving epidermal diary entries from a long-dead polar explorer and that she shed them like a birch tree.

5.

The snow fell transcendently, struck their faces. Oksana had not been this happy in many months. She sucked in the cold air, until she started to cough, then tried to stifle it before Sasha could threaten to put her in a cab. But when she glanced at Sasha she saw that her daughter was absorbed in her phone, looking for her brother's number because she refused to put it in her favorites. Sasha's worry about the snow was escalating—she wanted to reach Dima and have him pick them up in his car.

"You don't know how lucky you are," Oksana said.

Sasha looked up, peered over her glasses to which snow was sticking. "I know, I know. I'm lucky to have a brother. And a sister. It's true."

"No. You're lucky to have those little whatsits."

"The phone?—"

"All those messages! You have no idea. There was nothing like that in my day. Nothing!" She was on a role, clarity was abundant—seize the day!—but she didn't know what she meant, exactly, by her day and Sasha's day, and if the messages she meant were the ones on Sasha's phone or the ones that were appearing on her skin. She was confused, too, by a misalignment in which dreams and reality were overlaid. During the night, she had opened her eyes around

2:15 a.m. and placed her hand on the wall beside her bed, and the wall was not separate. She was the wall and it was her, and she could not explain it. The inanimate, she felt, had been misunderstood. Take Sasha's treatment of her devices, for instance, how she purposefully let their charges run down, or left them in sofa cracks or muffled in purses, cursed them, even poured water over their screens. To no avail, apparently, as the little machines, emitting their beeps and purrs, were ever present.

Sasha had returned to her phone. "Nothing is stopping you from having one. You keep refusing, remember?"

Oksana couldn't remember, which embarrassed her. Lapses in memory were something she tried to fudge over, often with a joke. "Well, time is up!"

"Okay."

"It was a lovely evening. It would be fine if I died tonight."

"All right."

6.

Sasha looked up from her phone because her mother grabbed her arm. Oksana made a little cry as she fell to the ground, landing hard on her knees. She was amazed at the force, how heavy she was, and helpless to the physics of it. Her body was supposed to be frail and brittle, but she fell like a redwood onto the salt-flecked concrete. Pain rushed through her from her knees straight up to her head. A couple walking nearby helped Sasha get Oksana to her feet, once she had caught her breath. It seemed that nothing was broken. One of the people suggested a cane or a walker as Sasha nodded and thanked them profusely. Oksana ignored them all and watched the snow fall around them, huge flakes that clung to eye-lashes, flew up nostrils. As they waited for Dima to come and get them, she opened her mouth as wide as she could until several landed on her tongue.

The dance halls.

1.

Where her husband wouldn't dance, and then the men who did. Oh, they loved her. How she moved, even though she was short and muscular, her chest too ample, but she smiled and coaxed in

a way that drew them toward her. The bad ones were her favorites, the ones who tried to hide their bulges with feigned politeness, knuckling their caps as if they were boys, but she saw how they skulked around her until one of them was brave enough to encroach. She almost never said no, not to a dance at least, her husband watching from the table, mild as a spring day, and inclined to asking her afterward how it was. What did Sasha, and Dima and Anna, know of her heart, any heart, and what did they know, really, about her mind. What it contained. What it mulled in the night when her hand was the wall was her hand was the world.

2.

In the morning, Oksana lay in her bed and watched the ceiling. Sometimes sleep swallowed who she was and a perilous sea rocked around her. The pieces came back slowly at first, a recognition of the dresser in the corner, the familiar blanket, then the bloom of her details in an instant and she knew her name again.

She recalled the night before, how she fell. Her body ached, but especially her knees. She saw that Sasha had placed both her cane and, even more vile, her walker, leftover from her husband, beside the bed. Her drapes were closed, so she could not see if it was still snowing, if rips of the sky still fell, surely big as birds. She felt her fingertips burn with the cold of the snow clusters, even as she lay in bed, and then the sensation was gone. It occurred to her that the problem was the interior view, the wrong side of the glass. Still in bed.

3.

A copy of Scott's journals that had belonged to her husband sat on her bedside table, fat with use and bookmarks. Her husband was an unexpected reader of polar adventure; unexpected because he had disliked anything athletic and hated the outdoors. She herself read the journals only to conjure him, to imagine his fingertips, like the feet of a rabbit, on the pages. She could not account for his interest in Scott's journey, though it struck her suddenly that it was Scott's death, the way he ended, that had interested him. *For God's sake, look after our people.* Perhaps her husband had been preparing himself, or taking notes, or commiserating. Or wishing.

4.

She wondered at her daughter's condition. When she noticed one of the skin tags on the floor the previous day, she covered it with her foot until Sasha left the room and she had the time to bend slowly, ever so slowly, and pick it up. Once she had it, she examined it under her magnifying glass.

it looked like a rough sea.

The words washed in and out of her own fulgurating sensations and memories, her looseness in the world. She did not think her daughter beautiful, not even as a baby, and she rarely complimented her, but what she held in her hand struck her as an object of great beauty; the words plaintive, and lonesome, but the thing itself was luminous and strange, and had somehow emerged from the being that was her peculiar daughter. When she heard Sasha taking a shower, she shuffled to the kitchen, found an empty jar, placed the message inside it, and carried it back to her room, where she hid it under the bed.

The visitors.

1.

"Have fun with Auntie and Oksana," Dima said. *"And no fighting,"* he hissed, then waved merrily at them all and departed. Beatrice was seven, and the youngest. Ella and Max were ten and twelve. They stood in the foyer in their coats and school uniforms, cold still clinging, and hugged Oksana, who had ambled over to receive them, and then they gaped at Sasha. She offered them hot chocolate, which made them dump their coats and boots and swarm the kitchenette. Max pulled open the cupboards, looking for the powdered mix while Ella, silently noting the ones still dirty in the sink, searched for mugs. "We should make it Mexican, with cayenne in it," said Max.

Beatrice, who had been sucking her middle fingers as she had done almost since birth, pulled them out and said, "I think your information is wrong. I don't think that's how they drink it."

Sasha tried to laugh merrily, while scooting them out of the way before somebody got burned or smashed a mug. She was not easily enamored of children the way that some people seemed to be, not even the ones related to her. And for their part, they disliked the brown hats she sometimes pulled down over her ears—

one of them called her Gnomeskull—or the jumpy way she had of talking while eating, so that crumbs showered around her and they stared aghast at the ball of food tucked half into her cheek. They did not know what to do with the silver dollars in plastic jackets she gave them or the oddly expensive pens. Still, she made them giggle, and she did not mind too much; she made them biscuits they pretended to nibble, she taught them to fold paper into miniscule cranes that had wild, brief flights before dropping dead in the waste basket.

"You look like purple Jacksons," Oksana said, beaming. Max, Ella, and Beatrice all turned and looked at her. Sasha was about to say something but Beatrice smiled and took Oksana's hand.

"Mama says you're dotty," she said, and laughed.

"Perfect," said Sasha, and turned to fill the kettle with water, sending some cutlery skittering across the counter.

Oksana placed her hands on Beatrice's cheeks. "Your mother's a witch, sweetheart. Pay no mind." Max burst out laughing and covered his mouth with his hand. Oksana was thoughtful. "But, then again, maybe she's right. I suppose I am."

Beatrice nodded vigorously. "Yes." The fingers went back in her mouth.

"The man who performed Einstein's autopsy made off with his brain," said Ella. "In a jar." She had a habit of piling her long hair, which always seemed to be damp, on top of her head and then unpiling it, over and over, and was now busy mounding it. "He sliced some of it up and put it on slides."

"Imagine that." Oksana walked slowly over to the sofa and settled herself into it. From this viewpoint, her favorite, she could see the snow falling outside the window. She clucked her tongue.

"Will you look at that. Again. Tremendous." Beatrice climbed up and sat nestled against her.

Sasha brought a tray of mugs and shortbread and set them on the coffee table in front of Oksana. A wave of itchiness trickled along her arm, a small spasm, and hot chocolate glugged onto the tray. "Oh, shoot." Max and Ella exchanged glances, *she's such a spaz!* Oksana heaved herself forward, which was sometimes a process of asking her brain to move her (always the mental image was smoother than the movement actually produced), to help wipe up the mess, but she was stopped by a glimmer on Sasha's wrist, a paper unfolding, grey-flecked and vaguely scabrous. Lust rumbled up in her almost audibly; how she wanted to grab it, read it, keep it. Outside there was a turmoil of crystals and wind—there was a tribe, she thought, somewhere, who said that a storm was a lost soul trying to find its way—and in here, the messages, snow-filled, plaintive. Coming through.

Ella saw it and made a face. "What is *that*?"

Sasha recoiled, and covered her wrist. "Excuse me," she said. "Nothing for you to worry over."

"I wasn't worried. You have a disease, Auntie!"

"Don't be silly."

Max's eyes burned with delight. "You do so, Auntie!" Beatrice started to cry.

"Oh, for Pete's sake," said Sasha. She couldn't help scratching; she was helpless to it. The paper fluttered down and Max reached for it, but it was Oksana who snatched it so quickly that Beatrice stopped wailing. They all watched Oksana, who put it in her mouth.

"That's just crazy," Max said, shaking his head and slowly stirring a spoon in his mug.

Ella was now flipping herself upside-down on the sofa so that her hair swept the floor. "Want to know the scientific term for brain freeze? It's *sphenopalatine ganglioneuralgia.*" She examined her feet, which were bare because she refused to wear socks, as they dangled high above her.

2.

In her bedroom, Oksana spit the message into her hand and carefully unraveled it. She could not find her glasses at first, and tried to picture them, where they might be. She had a few notes taped around her room, at Sasha's insistence, reminding her of certain

details, where her purse was, how many pills to take and when, the names of her children and their children, phone numbers, but no mention of the glasses. Finally, she found them on the desk underneath a scuba manual (no recollection of why she had that in her possession, though perhaps it was related to the dreams she had been having of being submerged in great expanses) and put them on.

Beautiful day—too beautiful—

She well knew the sentiment, the excessive goodness in certain sights could be painful. Holding tight to the message, she got down on her knees, *like an old moose* she thought, wincing with pain because of the bruises big as plums, and lifted the bedcover. Underneath the bed, quietly gleaming among the dust and hair tangles because she would not allow Sasha to vacuum her room, were the various empty jars she had fished out of the recycling bin and hoarded. She dropped the skin tag into one of the jars, holding it up to the light for a moment to see that it was like a coruscating fish, or better yet, she thought, snow. It had a luminosity that troubled and delighted her, a presence that spoke of things eternal and just beginning to be known to her.

Tongues.

1.

The snow was whipping again into a storm and it was expected to hover for days. Oksana sat again in the living room and watched it through the window. Snow had a transcendence born of microscopic, hard lines that appeared soft to the human eye. What kind of a trick! she thought. Marvelous. Out loud she said, "The mister who brought the mail should have brought candy." She laughed at the words; she had no idea what she meant.

Sasha knew better than to express alarm, or even to feel it. Clarity in her mother came and went, and the doctor said as much. You had to cope with the waves in their sequence, one by one, like a surfer. He was tan, and that was the comparison he'd used. Surfing was something she loved the thought of, but had never done. Perhaps she would get the chance, after her mother . . . She glanced at Oksana, wondering if she had spoken any of that aloud. Oksana was gazing into the distance, her fingers wrapped around a teacup. Except that her hands appeared to grip the cup too tightly.

Suddenly, Oksana was on her feet. Whatever soreness she had complained of earlier in the day seemed to be gone and she moved speedily around the corner, to the hall closet where her coat was stored. Sasha heard the clack of coat hangers and raced to catch her mother.

"What are you doing? Where are you going?" Sasha cried.

"Kipsnitch!" Oksana clutched her coat. "Kipsnitch!" She meant snow, snow goddammit. She waved her hands toward the door, toward the unknown world on the other side, because what, really, was there? She could not quite remember or make it out, except that snow was falling and she had to tilt her head back and feel the crystalline softness on her tongue. It was not enough to see it through the window pane; it had to be *experienced*. "Understand that!" she said.

"Well, I do understand," Sasha said. "You can't go out there.

It's freezing, it's dark, and there's ice everywhere. Even I could barely manage the sidewalk. What if you fell again?"

Oksana, still clutching her coat, stared at her daughter. Sasha winced at the brokenness on her face, a nakedness she had never seen, but it was fleeting. Oksana patted the coat that was folded over her arm, before Sasha took it from her, and walked unsteadily back into the living room.

2.

She began surreptitiously to watch her daughter, hoping to catch sight of a bit of lifting skin near her cuff or neck. (Once, when she did, she said cryptically, "Light hath no tongue, but is all eye," quoting Donne and startling Sasha.) Infrequently, Sasha even had one on her face, but she was likely to notice those and rip them off. The ones that appeared on her arms and legs were the ones most likely to drop without her knowledge, or become snagged inside a sweater, and if they fell on the carpet she was sometimes oblivious. These were the ones that Oksana fixed upon, tossing a magazine or tissue over the spot until she could make her way over to it. The problem was bending without attracting Sasha's concern.

The fallen snow crystals are quite feathery like thistledown.

and the crystals are minute.

—horrible light, which made everything look fantastic.

. . . the sandy snowdrifts similar to those on summit,

Wonders! She collected these over two days and placed them in the jars beneath her bed. The messages that had more to do with Scott's struggle she left lying on the ground for Sasha to find later.

Poor Wilson has a fearful attack of snow-blindness

Fuel is woefully short.

We talk of little but food, except after meals.

3.

She snuck into Sasha's room while Sasha was in the laundry room of the building. Neither of them could be called tidy, but Sasha sometimes wallowed in an intermittent messiness, confined mostly to her room, which had undusted blinds, water in various glasses and mugs, a trail of potato chip crumbs or nail clippings along the fringes of things, a prickly light. Oksana rummaged through the dresser, cracked open the closet door, even looked inside Sasha's handbag, which hung from a chair back and contained three dispensers of hand sanitizer, and none of the messages. Then she saw Sasha's planner on the desktop and one of the skin tags emerging from the pages. When she opened the planner, she found thirty-four of the messages, most of them noting Scott's ever-increasing disaster, the men's starvation, the frozen fingers and toes. She rooted through these while holding her magnifying glass in the other hand and chose:

the soft recently fallen snow clogging the ski and runners at every step,

where we had the four-day blizzard.

an hour after starting loose ice crystals spoiling surface.

Very curious surface—soft recent sastrugi which sink underfoot,

a sort of flaky crust with large crystals beneath.

All of which she smuggled to her room and placed in the jars. They glistened when she held them up. A vastness sloshed around her, and she felt the urge to lie down in it.

4.

Sometimes desire was a palpable entity, all gaping mouth and hands. How to measure the lust she felt for the little papers. She was sorry for Scott's plight, she was, but it was long past. The current storm, the one outside the apartment building, and which had already gone on for three days (and which Max had described to her on the telephone that morning as a giant marshmallow shitting itself without end), continued snowing over miles of buildings and streets and little neighborhood parks and straining the city's snow-removal budget. She had tried to convince Sasha that they should go out in it, even just to see, but Little Miss Know-Everything had simply waved her hand and gone back to peering into her laptop. A wonderful calamity was unfolding outside and her own daughter did not want any part of it.

———————

Little monsters.

1.

Sasha was researching skin diseases, but coming up with nothing. Marcus had rattled her when he phoned to ask, "Is it contagious, do you think?" She hung up on him, but found herself in front of her computer, scouring the internet. She went from photo to photo of the skin's inhabitants and diseases, sifted through the enlarged portraits of the creatures—monsters really—that mined the skin's surface, and bacteria that hustled among the follicles and epidermal cells, whole galaxies of atrocious blobs, articulated faces, antennae and claws tending to the boundary of what held her back from everything else.

2.

Disgusted, she briefly looked up Scott, but did not want to give him further attention, and anyway what she sensed existed on the other side of the messages was not a distressed man misplaced in time, but an emptiness so vast she sucked in her breath and went in search of some wine to open. Unscrewing the bottle, she considered that whatever entity or force was at work was driven not by a conviction that she was remotely special, but that she was simply an open target for random transmissions (compelling though the diaries may have been at one time, they were only more *blah blah blah*). She poured three inches of wine, drank, poured another. Two more messages dropped to the ground from inside her pant leg, and she felt another catch inside her underwear. She wondered if she should worry about attrition at a pace too fast for her body to keep up. The transmissions fell and sometimes they stuck to her shoes, so that it seemed she was perpetually stepping out of a porta-potty, dragging tissue.

3.

The storm was convenient, in a way. She was reluctant to leave the apartment on account of her condition and the weather was a good foil. The grocery store was only one block down and still doing deliveries, and the power had stayed on so far. She worried about Oksana, however, if something happened to her, if she needed a doctor quickly; she wondered, too, about Oksana's obsession with the snow, and, worse, with being outside in it. She was able to assuage the desire somewhat by heaving the recliner over to the window where her mother could look out from a more comfortable vantage than the sofa. She placed a pillow and blankets there for her, along with a little table and tray where Oksana could corral her water, her whiskey, her celebrity magazines, and a Mozart score (Requiem in D Minor) that she had been pretending to notate in raging, uncertain pencil. Still, Sasha sensed the inadequacy and that a

burgeoning, intoxicated desire seemed to swagger around Oksana if she got talking about the weather. She reminded herself
that her mother had never been easy to please. Just ask her
father.

———————

Gypsies.

1.

Oksana set up camp in the recliner around eleven p.m. on the
third night of the storm and remained there till morning. She
had everything she needed, including a single jar, in which
she had smuggled a dozen of the best snow messages, tucked in
the space between her hip and the chair. During the night, she
retrieved it, finding that her hands felt large and clumsy, held it
up a few times, examined it, replaced it next to her hip. She had
grown used to being stiff and sore and sleeping in increments,
but she enjoyed waking to see the snow that clung to the window. It blew in small tempests against the building, and burst
somehow from the starless sky. Between three and four a.m., she
was visited by the gypsy moths that flourished one summer day
when she stood on the road outside the house with the children,
Anna still in a stroller, Dima a toddler, and Sasha wearing one of
her hats even then, even on a hot day, as the moths pelted against
them; she beat back at them as the children squealed, shooing
the weird little creatures that were so bent on smashing themselves against human arms and legs. How she could almost feel
them again, there in Sasha's apartment. She was clear, she was
certain of that.

2.

In the morning, she woke and Sasha was bending over her and let out a little, "Oh!"

"I'm still here," Oksana said, though her voice was thick and slow. She fumbled for her water glass and Sasha helped her. "Stop! Mine to do."

"Fine, fine." Sasha went to the window and looked out at the snow piled on the roofs and balconies of the buildings across the street, the obliterated storefront signs down below. Someone was skiing down the middle of the street. "It's almost over."

3.

She saw Oksana look at the rug where a message had tumbled. She hadn't even felt an itch. She picked it up, sensed its difference even before squinting at it.

"What does it say?" Oksana said.

Sasha handed it to her. "I know you've been taking them. You can have it."

Oksana put her glasses on and selected her magnifier from the tray beside her. She hummed as she tried to see the print, but something was wrong. The message appeared to be wordless, a tiny blank. "Nothing," she said quietly. "Did we miss it?"

"Did we miss what?"

"Oates. The poor chap who went off to die alone in the snow. What did he say? 'I am just going outside and may be some time.'"

"How are you able to remember that? There was one last night, right before I got into bed." She pulled it out of her pocket.

It seems a pity, but I do not think I can write more.

"Huh," Oksana said, chagrined. "That is the end of it, then."

Sasha dared to feel some relief; perhaps it was true, that it was over. She felt, when she thought about it, calm and restful. Itchless. Oksana was obviously stricken, as if by a terrible loss, and she stared out the window where the few remaining flakes were not the giants of the night before but anemic and lazily falling. She wondered if her mother had intended to copy Oates in some way, to wander out into the snow and be claimed by it. "I'll run a bath for you," she said. "And we'll go out somewhere for lunch."

4.

In the evening Oksana lay in her bed with Scott's journals on her chest, rising and falling as she breathed. "You poor bastard," she whispered, though she was unsure if she meant Scott or her husband. If her husband was there in the room with her, Sasha wondered what would she say to him. What he would say to her. *Life is long,* he always used to say. Perhaps she would tell him about the walls, how they disappeared sometimes. Perhaps she would tell Sasha about them. Death was an error in thinking that people fell into, a philosophical pothole that swallowed them. You staggered along with your companions until they disappeared, one by one. Belief was the catalyst, therefore, the cause and then its effect. She said, *I'm going to die tonight*, but what she meant was: *I will never die*. She could not always explain the errors in translation from her mind to her mouth.

Canst thou not cease,
inventive as
thou art
And subtle, from the wiles
which
thou hast lov'd
Since thou wast infant, and from
tricks of speech
Delusive, even in thy native land?

—HOMER, *THE ODYSSEY*

ACKNOWLEDGMENTS

Thank you to Laurie Grassi, my editor at Simon & Schuster Canada, for being such a splendid reader and adviser, and the voice on the other end of the line; my agent and friend, Nathaniel Jacks, of InkWell Management, New York City; my early readers and supporters, Ron MacLean, Marjan Kamali, Ilan Mochari, Sarah Gerkensmeyer, Patti Hall, and Patricia Magosse.

Thanks also to the editors at *Alaska Quarterly Review* (especially Ron Spatz), *The Normal School*, *Guernica*, *SmokeLong Quarterly*, and *Juked* for publishing early versions of some of these stories; to Jonathan Cott for permission to use parts of his wonderful interview with Glenn Gould; and to the Glenn Gould Foundation. Kevin Bazzano's biography on Gould, *Wondrous Strange*, was a tremendous resource.

Much of my enjoyment in doing research for the stories came from reading fairy tale and fable history, especially *Little Red Riding Hood Uncloaked*, by Catherine Orenstein, and *Secrets Beyond the Door*, by Maria Tatar. Gratitude, also, for the countless short-story writers whose work it was a joy to immerse myself in, for the inspirations that came from them, particularly Gabriel García Márquez's story "The Very Old Man with Enormous Wings."

Most of all, to my husband, Robin, and sons, Gabriel and Samuel: immense love.

PERMISSIONS AND CREDITS

"The Peregrine at the End of the World" appeared in *Alaska Quarterly Review* (thirty-fifth anniversary issue).

"Phone Booth" appeared in *The Normal School*.

"Appetites" appeared in *Guernica*, as well as their print anthology *Guernica Annual 2014*.

"Sea of Love" appeared (in shorter form) in *SmokeLong Quarterly*.

"Kites" appeared in *Juked*.

Acknowledgment is made to Jonathan Cott for permission to reprint excerpts from his book *Conversations with Glenn Gould* © Jonathan Cott.

ABOUT THE AUTHOR

Robin Wilson

Maria Mutch is a Canadian writer whose memoir, *Know the Night*, was a finalist for both the Governor General's Literary Awards and the Kobo Emerging Writer Prize, and was listed in *The Globe and Mail*'s Top 100 and *MacLean's* Best Reads. Her writing has appeared in *Guernica*, *The Malahat Review*, and *Poets & Writers*. She lives in Rhode Island with her husband and two sons. Visit her at www.mariamutch.com or follow her on Twitter @maria_mutch.

A NOTE ON THE TYPE

This book was set in Dante, a typeface originally designed by Giovanni Mardersteig shortly after the Second World War. Redrawn for digital use and given a range of weights by Monotype's Ron Carpenter, Dante creates harmony between the roman and the italic, and has the characteristic beauty of Renaissance typefaces.

The sans serif typeface used for titles and headings in this work is Brandon Grotesque, designed by Hannes von Döhren. Inspired by sans serif fonts of the 1920s and '30s, Brandon Grotesque's rounded corners lend warmth to the normally stark typefaces of this era.